Books by Gretchen Finletter

FROM THE TOP OF THE STAIRS

THE DINNER PARTY

THE
 DINNER PARTY

THE

DINNER PARTY

(From the Journal of a Lady of Today)

GRETCHEN FINLETTER

New York　　Atheneum　　*1981*

Library of Congress Cataloging in Publication Data

Finletter, Gretchen Damrosch.
    The dinner party (from the journal of a lady of today)

    I. Title.
PS3511.I584D5   1981   813'.54   81-3517
ISBN 0-689-70611-1   AACR2

Published simultaneously in Canada by
McClelland and Stewart, Ltd.
Manufactured by Fairfield Graphics, Fairfield, Pennsylvania
First Atheneum Edition

To
T. K. F.

# CONTENTS

THE
 *DINNER PARTY*

MAY

May 4

The trouble with rich friends is that they are so expensive.

This thought unfortunately only occurs to me after I have suggested that we have the Pullmans to dinner, as they are at least two years overdue. I make the mistake of bringing this all up at luncheon on a Saturday when both children are there.

Charles, who is born hospitable, says, Of course, high time, by all means, why not? The 'why not' makes me immediately against the idea as the Pullmans live grandly and I know that I will find myself trying to evolve a dinner that will appear equally grand. I decide that I will not discuss this aspect before Rachel and little Cissie as it will give them the wrong values, plus a poor impression of me.

Charles goes on to say it must be small, not more than eight, so we can have General Conversation. This is an obsession of Charles which in my experience only produces a monologue by Host or Feature Player, with expressions on the faces of the other guests of frightened anticipation that they will be called on for well-rounded opinions, or hurt feelings if they are not. I suggest that we can bury the Pullmans better with twelve, whereupon Cissie, who is I am afraid rather morbid, looks startled, puts both elbows on the table, rests her chin in her hands, and listens intently.

Charles then says that that is what I always do—get nervous, lack confidence, and invite too many people, and one ends without getting the good out of anyone. Hadn't I read him that account just the other day of Somerset Maugham refusing any invitation where there were to be more than seven? (Do not see how S. Maugham knows from an invitation how many there will be, but presume like royalty his wishes are understood in all the capitals of the world.)

I argue that if we are going to have all the fuss of getting up a dinner, we might as well be hung for a sheep as a lamb. Why not Kill Off a few people? Cissie starts breathing through her mouth. Charles remarks that we mustn't jump the gun with anyone else until the Pullmans are well nailed down. Cissie breathes more loudly. And anyhow, continues Charles, he finds Pullman an interesting man in his own way. He is Chairman of the E.L.O. Company which controls the I.J.S. which has amalgamated with Gloss Copper, and Charles had heard he is due for a big appointment in Washington, which is quite remarkable as five years ago E.L.O. had tried to kick him upstairs. As Charles says this he laughs, whereupon Cissie, her eyes welling with tears, says you are all cruel to poor Mr. Pullman (whom I do not think she has ever seen) and rushes from the table. Rachel automatically says Cry-baby, and Charles, aghast, asks what has happened.

We continue, and finally agree on a compromise of ten, of which two besides the Pullmans as a concession to me may be Kill-Offs. I then suggest that we begin by trying to get a single man as that will give us something to play with, and will be not only a spare tire, but an ace in the hole, and good insurance. There are always of course Dr. Harden and Mr. Case, but couldn't Charles for once make that his department and find a New Single Man. Just for once try to produce an attractive, new . . .

Charles asks why I am getting so excited, that of course he will get someone, and I am left stunned with surprise and gratitude. Rachel then says Please ask the two Miss

Putnams because they told her the other day they never get invited anywhere, and never never see any men. I say Not this time; some day later, and ask Charles what we shall have to eat. Charles says, For God's sake, not Ham, and why not pheasant? Also he will arrange to get Old Tom from the Golf Club to help with the drinks, but then it must not be a Saturday night when Tom is busy.

Rachel then repeats, Please ask the two Miss Putnams because they are so poor. I say Hush and she adds Why do we give pheasants to the Pullmans who are so rich anyhow. It isn't Fair. Charles says Please shut up and Rachel adds that this is not true Democracy and Miss Licks her teacher says that Thomas Jefferson, where she is At now, always asked everyone for every meal, and to stay for weeks and weeks, and that in a real Democracy . . .

I interrupt to say that Jefferson was lucky because he had lots and lots of slaves, and I wish I had, whereupon Rachel howls that it is simply awful to believe in slavery, and even if she is not At the Civil War yet, she certainly knows that Jefferson would have asked the two Miss Putnams to a dinner party, and in a real Democracy Miss Licks says . . .

Charles cries Break it up, Rachel, and let's have coffee outside. We postpone further talk on dinner party and Charles says that Linda is his only daughter who has turned out well, and why did she have to choose a college so far away. I agree Linda is the apple of, and decide not to bring up other problems now.

(Ponder to myself Rachel's statement on hospitality of T. Jefferson which I know was fabulous, but wonder why one never knows in history how the wives felt. Realize in all honesty that I cannot remember if there was a Mrs. J. Intend to look this up, but know probably will not do so for some time.)

May 6

The plans for dinner party move ahead, but undergo a deep sea change. Mrs. Pullman and Mr. P. can only come on a Saturday (Old Tom therefore excluded) and she will let me know who will be with them—probably an odd man. I try to sound nonchalant about this last possibility, but am afraid my voice betrays me.

She repeats she will let me know, soon, and then asks if Charles is better? I say he has never been ill, but is writing a Book. Mrs. Pullman exclaims that oh she knew we had left the city and is glad to hear it was for nothing serious. (Cannot decide if this is humor.) I in return inquire about Mr. Pullman, and Mrs. P. informs me that she never sees him these days as of course he is so much in Washington. I say Of course rather respectfully, and kick myself for it. (Wonder why I always do this? Think it is a desire to be popular.)

Mrs. P. then asks after the little girls, calling them by wrong names which it does not seem worth while to correct. I inquire about her daughter, using the right name, Olivia, and Mrs. Pullman tells me she is well but under a fearful nervous strain due to impending examinations at her school. Olivia is brilliant, exceptionally so, but alas no student.

We again repeat date, hour, Black Tie, and she will let me know, in Plenty of Time.

The other Kill-Offs, known as my Concession, are the Lawlers, long overdue, who accept. Charles having pleaded that we have at least one person we like, I ask the Tracys, and even go so far as to explain the whole situation to Maud, and tell her that she and Hick are the only couple we really want. Maud replies that she kills off with cocktails, period, and would never waste a dinner on Lawlers or Pullmans. I then hear myself telling her that George Pullman is an interesting man about to take a big post in Washington. Maud answers that she is surprised that impresses a Democrat like me, and I answer that I call myself an Independent with Democratic leanings, which produces only a cackle from Maud. She then says that Saturday is a hard night to get extra help and she might, but only might, be able to loan me her Annie. Will have to see. I tell her this will Solve Everything, and she promises she will let me know.

Charles then produces his surprise. He has telephoned to reactivated Army Base thirty-four miles away, and invited General McQuinn, whom he has met once. He is, says Charles, a two-star West Pointer, and handsome. I am quite overcome. Has he accepted? No, but Charles has spoken to his aide who says the General has nothing laid on and will telephone us later.

I go into happy anticipatory dream of effect on Maud when glittering General marches in. It then appears relatively safe (with Pullman odd man and General) to ask extra woman, and extend invitation to Mary Singer who is not only Head of distinguished Girls' School, and great Brain, but—surprisingly—attractive. Miss Singer says she rests on week ends but as I have said it will be small, she will come. She and I have after all that bond of having worked for Stevenson, and flatteringly she wants to hear what I think now.

When I tell this to Charles (who voted for Eisenhower for the usual reasons) he begs me not to turn the evening into a political brawl, the election is over, and why not let the dead bury their dead. This extraordinary statement I cannot let pass and we find ourselves in a near brawl, only to be interrupted by the telephone.

There is a click and a crackle and a masculine voice says 'Connect with Quarters One.' Then buzzing and signals and another voice announces 'Sergeant Tremont, Quarters

One.' First voice says 'Ready on call placed by Major Sylvester at thirteen hours for General McQuinn, party on wire.' 'Yes Sir,' responds Sergeant Tremont. I prepare a very charming smile which wipes itself off my face when a soft voice says, 'Hulloa there, this is Dolly McQuinn.' I reply 'Oh yes,' meaning Oh NO! 'The General and I will be pleased to accept your kind invitation to dinner, and will it be Formal?'

I put hand over mouthpiece and say to Charles, Married! and then express delight and say it's a small dinner party (which it is no longer) and Black Tie. Then think of General's uniform which I at all costs want, but do not know how to phrase in military terms. Dolly then states she has a short evening dress, formal at the 'top' and with a jacket. I say How lovely—start to give road directions and Dolly cries Oh the Aide will take care of that. Then have Brain Storm, or Stroke of Genius, and ask her if Major Sylvester is married. Heavens, no, replies Dolly, an Aide is no good if he's married. Would he possibly enjoy also—? Certainly. She will bring him. (Order him?) My opinion of Dolly is now extremely high, and as I hang up I reflect that hard as the life in the Armed Services must be, it has certain remarkable compensations.

Charles, after the fiasco of the marital status of the General, admits I have been adroit and I go into happy fantasy that if Major Sylvester proves attractive, can get him over again when dear Linda returns. (Must stop this tendency toward Day Dreams, as not one has ever come true.)

May 8

Plans for dinner interrupted by first estimate on small portion of contemplated alteration of house, which staggers Charles and which I refuse to even look at, until party is behind me.

Charles however will not let it go and says if this is an example of what is to come, he is for giving up the whole idea of the country, and moving back to the city. I say we have sublet the apartment and what about the Book? Charles says the book is probably no good, and I say I Know It Is. Charles asks how I can know since I have only read three chapters. I say I loved those chapters, whereupon Charles replies that one does not 'love' a broad analysis of Foreign Policy and World Economic Conditions. I also add that I want to read more, but it is difficult when there are so many Riders clipped on, and things crossed out. Wait till it's all neatly typed.

Charles points out that I am merely trying to divert him from the estimate. He finally agrees to put it in wire basket on desk, face down for ten days, and we have a cocktail.

May 12

Party now completely out of hand and adds up to at least fifteen. Mrs. Pullman telephones that she is overjoyed to hear that the Bromleys are going to be with them—of course I know who they are—and she will bring them. They always contribute so. I again approach the Odd Man. Mrs. Pullman does not understand what I am referring to. The names, she repeats, are Mr. and Mrs. Estabrook Bromley.

Long-distance call from my sister Julie whom I thought in Europe, screaming that she has just landed and will be right up for a visit. Cissie and Rachel shout with joy and ask if she is bringing them presents. Charles also expresses pleasure, and I feel I will sound unaffectionate if I refer to extra man problem in relation to Julie.

Later I suggest we make dinner a Buffet and Charles says this is the last straw. He has never been to a buffet which was not confused and messy. I then give him a vivid description of new-type buffet, a half-and-half, with bottles of wine on tables, which I have read about and even seen pictures of—in color, and then spoil my account by saying of course pheasant is out and it looks like Ham.

Charles asks how he is supposed to concentrate on his book if he has to consider these petty details. He then adds for God's sake not to stick around that Chilean wine in black bottles, left over from the War Years. He will take care of the wine—leave that at least to him.

It is not the moment to remind him of the cavity left by Old Tom.

May 15

Make up my mind to be clear-headed and authoritative and write out on pad what I plan to have for dinner party. Will then go into kitchen and simply Tell Roza. Rehearse conversation. Must not begin with 'Oh by the way, Roza, we are having a few people in,' which is cowardly, nor 'Give me your suggestions, Roza,' which is craven, but go into kitchen, say 'Good morning,' bring out my pad and list, and tell her, pleasantly of course, that we are going to have a small dinner of about eighteen people.

(Find I am talking into the mirror and the face that looks out at me resembles Uriah Heep.)

Decide instead to go to Mary Jane's Beauty Shoppe. Know it is several days before the party but do not wish Mrs. Pullman to imagine that the dinner is so important to me that my hair has been especially waved for it, and feel it is more worldly to have it on the night either a bit over-ripe or under-done. Will have to produce this effect by brushing it hard, or not combing it at all for five days.

Antie, who sits behind the desk at Mary Jane's and whose

curls are bright blue, reproaches me for not having been to them in a long time and says that from one quick glance she can see that I desperately need a cream shampoo.

I disappear into the booth where Antie's daughter Heloise shows me a series of pictures on a large card and asks if I do not wish to be restyled. Heloise has only recently returned from a Hairdressers' and Cosmetologists' Convention where she took a refresher course of two hours, and can now do the New Look. I inquire which of the pictures represents the Look as they vary from Psyche to Marlon Brando.

Antie joins us and points to a mature type whose head is a mass of swirls and announces to Heloise that that is me, and don't I want a manicure. I ask their opinion of the Italian cut, and Antie says it looks like dirty hair hacked with a nail scissors, and not for her, no thank you.

Finally agree to manicure, but prevail that my hair shall be done 'the old way.' Close my eyes and Antie mutters something about 'facial for tired lines.' Pretend not to hear, and eventually loud dryer cuts off communication and only audible words to reach me are 'Duchess of Windsor nail polish like all the ladies of your age.' Decide that Antie is an old blue pussy-cat.

On arrival home Rachel says Oh you have had your hair washed, Why, and then adds casually that Roza has been stumping around for hours as she wants to Talk to me.

With prophetic foreboding know that this is to give notice as it is euphemistically called, and I can see she has so timed it that she can comfortably catch the afternoon train. Debate whether I shall interrupt Charles, which I have promised never to do except for Long Distance or an accident.

Recall that hopeful period when I had dreamed that Roza might fall in love with Charles, which friends have told me is the only way nowadays to hold anyone. But in three months have seen no evidence of a rising passion on Roza's part, though in the first few weeks had urged Charles to go into the kitchen and alternate between praise and jollying along.

Find myself speculating that if Charles had fallen in love with Roza, considering impending dinner, would I not have been more than acquiescent? Am quite shocked at my morbid fancies yet feel this could be a theme for poignant tragi-comedy.

March out toward kitchen with reproachful look already planted on my face, and run head on into Roza in Library who says she hears I am giving a dinner of twenty-six. Before I can make my denial, she adds she has already reserved a salmon. The relief is too great, I find my eyes full of hysterical tears, and I sink to the sofa. Roza joins me on it and I show her pictures of new-type buffet, in color. Roza says it looks Krazy, like old restaurant in Pest.

Later describe episode to Charles, slanting it to sound as

though only extraordinary diplomacy on my part had made Roza change her mind and remain with us. Charles says it is obvious that as a small child I must have been bitten by a cook, and the marks still show.

Find Cissie in my bedroom behind the curtain by the window. Inquire what she is looking out at, and she says Nothing. Sound her out if she had fun at school today, and she says it was all right. Has she a pain anywhere? No. Then she gives a deep sigh. Cannot see her clearly because of large pink roses on chintz curtain.

Finally Cissie emerges and asks if she can have a friend called Louise, from her school in the city, come up and visit her for a week. I cannot recall Louise nor can Cissie identify her beyond saying that she was in her group in the second term. Cissie then adds that she has had a letter from Louise, and Louise has indicated she would like to come.

I suggest that we wait until after the dinner before writing Louise, and Cissie, looking much relieved, runs out of the room.

Go into the library and peek at estimate of intended alteration. Know I have agreed with Charles we should postpone mutual study but wish to prepare myself for what I would like to save out of inevitable cuts. (Find that in arguments of money versus desire, I often lose because of lack of clarity of financial terms and inability to do quick subtraction.)

Am even more aghast than Charles at final total on fifth page. Can see a struggle forming between necessity and aesthetics, and debate with myself whether quick generous insistence that plan for four new bookshelves in bedroom for Charles must go through will get response that wall knocked down between small parlor and old dark hall shall not be canceled.

May 17

Drive twenty-two miles to town where there is small store which calls itself a Food Specialty Shoppe, but is actually a rather inferior Delicatessen.

De Boss, as he is called, says he has been saving something just for me as I am the only lady in these parts who understands cheese. He then hauls out a hunk of green veined marble, molding at one side, and whispers it is genu-ine import, just arrived—smell it, and, pulling out a knife—taste it.

I cannot taste it, but say I will buy a quarter of a pound. De Boss is horrified. Let such an opportunity go by! I am mad if I do not take it all. He hauls it on the scale, names a large sum, and says for me he will knock off fifty cents. But steel has at last entered my spirit and I say half a pound or nothing.

De Boss groans, shakes his head, and cuts the cheese.

He then turns around smiling, asks about the leetle Bambinos, carries out the rest of my order which he places in the back seat of the car, but puts the cheese close to me.

May 19

Maud telephones that I can have her Annie, but Annie has stipulated she will under no circumstances go into the kitchen as she does not like Roza because of her religion. (As Roza has never asked to go to Church can only assume it is because of her lack of it.) Maud then adds that Hick will drive Annie over Saturday in the afternoon.

I am overcome at this gesture of Hick's, and I tell Maud that I know Charles would never do anything so thoughtful. Maud agrees that he would not and then adds that someday he may have to. Can see there will come a return engagement, and I will have to contribute my pounds of flesh.

Secure Mrs. Biltz from village who cleans and will go into kitchen or anywhere else but only if she can bring along her cat. As Mrs. Biltz does not mind walking, I agree to cat and warn Rachel and Cissie that Taffy and Old Joe must be shut upstairs.

Invite Dr. Harden who to my surprise cannot come, so fall back on Mr. Case, who of course can. Am aware that he will be the symbol to Maud and the Lawlers that I have

scraped the barrel. Decide I will place him next to Mrs.
Estabrook Bromley with the faint hope that she will think
he is an exciting new man.

Ask Charles if he feels it would be very deceitful if I pretend to Julie that we have arranged this dinner party in
her honor. Charles says (rather smugly) that he has never
found that deceit pays in small matters and then adds that
anyhow Julie would find out because the children would
talk, particularly Rachel who is a kind of Gestapo.

This conversation interrupted by telephone and it is
Julie, who though aware of modern inventiveness still thinks
that Long Distance demands that the voice must carry the
extra mileage. She shouts that she is delayed, something has
come up, and she will arrive Sunday or Monday. I tell her
that she will miss an enormous dinner we are giving just
for her. Julie suggests I postpone it and Charles, who is
sitting on the porch but hears Julie clearly, exclaims that
he would like to cancel the whole business. Julie then says
that she is appalled that we have gone to so much trouble,
aren't we darlings, but what can she do? Charles calls she
can hang up, she is on Long Distance, and does she know
the rates have gone up? Julie cries that some man is trying
to cut in, she cannot hear me, and will telephone again on
Sunday.

Later in the evening after Charles has gone to bed, start
moving furniture about to see if I can produce the effect

I am after. On third attempt at grouping, decide to put two tables in larger living room, and make long table in hall into buffet. Get this well under way, pushing sofas against walls, and am quite delighted with what I am achieving, when Charles appears in his wrapper and wants to know what I am making all the noise about, and do I know it is one-thirty?

I explain my plan, and Charles asks why we cannot eat in the dining room. This arrangement I assure him will have a kind of charm and will make everyone feel informal and gay, but as I say this I recognize that five of the guests I have never laid eyes on, and who knows what will *égayer* them. Charles looks more and more depressed, and to sugar the pill I add that if he will imagine he is at a jolly restaurant, then at his table he can have General Conversation, while at my table we can tête-à-tête.

Charles says that if I am going to try to move the piano now he might as well help me, which he does, and then we agree it looks better in its old corner, so we shove it back again. I go to the pantry and bring back some beer which we drink, each at his own table. I ask Charles if he does not now see how amusing it will be, but he gives me so bleak a look I see that it is indeed time to go to bed.

THE DINNER PARTY

May 21

At four in the afternoon as I am upstairs pressing my dress, I see Hick drive up in his sports roadster with Annie by his side. Annie steps out carrying a small valise, and I speculate as to why on a journey of four miles she has to wear a traveling costume, and cannot arrive already uniformed for the evening. Annie marches in through the front door and disappears, heaven knows where, to her dressing room. At the same moment with a roar of a throttle wide open, a motorcycle sweeps up, with a sidecar, out of which steps a khaki lieutenant. He is about to ring the bell when from around the corner appears Mrs. Biltz leading a cat, who has a collar on, by a chain.

The Lieutenant and Mrs. Biltz fall into low conversation, as he looks at the cat, and she is obviously having a hard time convincing him of something, but finally with a last skeptical look at the house, he jumps into the sidecar and bang-bangs off. Mrs. Biltz takes the path to the back door with pussy.

Two hours before anyone is expected I go downstairs, fully dressed (hair brushed hard), and encounter Charles with Rachel and Cissie, carrying bottles. Rachel and Cissie are doubling for Old Tom, and Charles has agreed that Cissie may wear her Spanish costume—a gift from Julie— but without the tambourine.

The plot of the buffet is unveiled for Annie and Mrs.

Biltz, and Annie views it with the same pessimism as Charles; Mrs. Biltz makes only two statements—that she hates to pass, and that that Cissie is sure a cute bag of tricks.

I visit the kitchen, which is quite smoky, and say to Roza, who is crouched on her knees in front of the oven, that it all smells delicious. Roza does not reply so I add that I know everything is going to be wonderful. (Would feel more secure if this assurance came from her.)

Roza finally turns and says that yellow is my color. Am once again overcome by beautiful yet surprising nature of Roza. Would like to urge her to come up and look at flower- and candelabra-bedecked buffet but do not wish there to be an early encounter with Annie. Tell her Mrs. Biltz will bring in the food, whereupon Roza says she will attend to that, no butterfingers on her dishes. See that meeting with Annie inevitable and can only hope that like old Troupers the show will go on. Give Roza a last warning that dinner may be a little delayed because of cocktails, and she asks rhetorically at what dinner has it ever been otherwise?

Return to the big hall and find Charles with Rachel and Cissie still hurling bottles about so that what was intended to be a scene of elegance, and somewhat like an interior Conversation Piece of the nineteenth century, now resembles a rather arty speakeasy.

THE DINNER PARTY

Ask Charles how he likes my dress and he says it looks all right. Ask if he cannot say anything more, and he finally remarks that it is a little top-heavy. I indignantly inquire what he means as the whole point is its simplicity and he answers he still thinks it would look better with less fruit. After two more wounding statements I take in that he is discussing the buffet, and agree with him that there are too many grapes in one bowl. By then it is too late to re-introduce the subject of my appearance.

At ten minutes to eight, just as I am lighting all the candles in all rooms, there is the bell. I say to Charles I am sure it is Mr. Case, which it is. After a quick glance about, Mr. Case exclaims that he sees we have begun our alteration and he admires us for having a dinner at this time. What spirit! He then spies the buffet around the corner and cries How utterly charming—it is like a Grandma Moses print. As there are spring flowers everywhere and I myself have given the silver so high a polish that it is almost blue, I find this remark singularly inappropriate.

We move into the smaller sitting room, where there is a fire lit which shines on the French andirons and pale brocaded portieres, and I wait to have it recall to Mr. Case the *Salle d'Attente* at the Gare St. Lazare, but he is too absorbed in explaining to Charles how to make 'my kind of cocktail.' This is described as weak, weak, but I observe that when Charles inquires if that is about right, Mr. Case suggests perhaps a finger or two more of Bourbon which eventually Rachel hands to him. He then, with a glance at Rachel, tosses over his shoulder to me that he can see that there is a certain somebody in this room who is destined to be a little heart-breaker, at which Rachel gives a rather silly smile.

There is a further flurry in the hall and I can hear Maud and Hick greeting Annie as though they had not seen her in years. They are followed by the Lawlers, and Beatrice Lawler, whom I have never thought of as particularly perceptive, exclaims over and over again that it is all too too divine and she couldn't be more impressed.

The bell rings again (I making a mental note that it is too loud and at least in the alteration we can afford a softer tone) when I see Charles go out, and hear voices preponderantly masculine. Charles then ushers in The General and Mrs. McQuinn, followed by Major Sylvester. The General and the Major are in uniform with many ribbons across their chests, and the General is indeed handsome. Mrs. McQuinn is blonde and pink and smiling, and wears an orchid.

The effect on Maud and Beatrice is electric as I nonchalantly assume that of course they have met General and Mrs. McQuinn and the Major—which I know full well they have not—and Mrs. McQuinn impresses me by repeating each name clearly as I make the introductions; tells Cissie she has a youngster who has a Hawaiian costume, and that Cissie and Rachel, again putting the right name on the right child, must come over to the Post and visit with her.

Major Sylvester, who resembles an exceptionally bright squirrel looped by a gold fourragère, immediately assists Charles with the cocktails. He is a veritable Old Tom in his efficiency, disappears to the pantry and returns with a coke with which he makes a drink on the rocks with a curling lemon peel for Mrs. McQuinn. He instinctively knows that Mr. Case is anxiously waiting for another cocktail, and hands it to him at full strength. He prepares the General's drink with great rapidity and at the same time keeps up a lively conversation with Beatrice Lawler, who has planted herself in that unassailable position of attraction—next to the ice bucket.

Again the bell tolls, and Cissie, who has moved on guard out front, announces to me in a whisper that it is poor Mr. Pullman.

The Pullmans with the Bromleys march in and the room immediately seems very crowded as all four are extremely large. Mrs. Pullman is in gray chiffon with a great many pearls, and Mrs. Bromley is exceptionally smart in black and white, which emphasizes the silvered streak in her black hair. She tells Charles in a penetrating voice she is simply terrified as she hears he is writing a book. This casts a momentary pall over everyone until Mr. Bromley cries that it takes all sorts to make a world, old man, doesn't it, and he wants a straight Scotch.

Mr. Pullman immediately gravitates toward the General and leads him three feet outside the circle where he engages him in solemn conversation with a portentous look on his face. As the General has been invented by Charles, find I resent this kidnaping by Mr. Pullman so early in the evening. Beatrice Lawler however quickly joins them, to the apparent pleasure of the General and frustration of Mr. Pullman.

Annie now appears to signal that dinner is ready and I signal not yet—one more, and two minutes later Mary Singer walks in, looking charming in a plum-colored dinner dress and infinitely younger than any of her contemporaries, largely due I think to her beautiful carriage and relaxed manner.

Introductions are made, and suddenly I see an expression like consternation on the face of Mrs. Pullman as she shakes Miss Singer's hand. I am at a loss to understand this and am further confused when I see her trying to attract the attention of Mr. Pullman, who has however again captured the General and propelled him away from Beatrice Lawler, to a small sofa near the door.

I ask Mrs. Pullman if she wants anything (sounding like a floorwalker) and she says she knows it is an odd question but is her husband by any chance to be placed near Miss Singer? I tell her I am pleased to say they are at the same table, as I am sure two such intelligent people—how easily it drips off my tongue—will enjoy each other.

Yes, yes, cries Mrs. Pullman, of course, how true, but she wants to get word to her husband that Miss Singer is The Miss Singer who is the principal of the school Olivia attends. Olivia—and Mrs. Pullman lowers her voice—has been having a little difficulty and she would not want George at this point to be in any way tactless. . . . Charles has now advanced toward Mrs. McQuinn and I leave Mrs. Pullman to deliver her singular message as best she can, as we all follow Charles and Mrs. McQuinn in to dinner.

The General, who is seated next to me, proves immediately to be an old Pro and makes himself agreeable within three seconds. He wants to know where I have been all his life. I remind him—the likeness is marked—of a woman, an outstanding beauty, he once knew back in Nanking. Have I been married before? He could swear he has seen me somewhere—now could it have been in Manila? There were many pretty girls there and he never forgets a face.

I find this delightful and am only too willing to trace our first acquaintance to the time he ruled Babylon and I was a mere slave, when Mr. Pullman who is on my other side booms in. He wants to ask the General a question, just one question, and if our charming hostess will forgive him, he thinks it will interest our whole table.

The General immediately assumes an intent expression and Mrs. Bromley cries How simply fascinating. Mr. Case attempts to look profound which merely makes him appear anxious, and Joe Lawler quickly fills his glass from one of the bottles against what may be a long drought. Mary Singer fixes her calm gaze on Mr. Pullman, and I refuse to catch Maud Tracy's eye.

What Mr. Pullman wishes to know, and he will state it in simple terms, what he would like to have from the General, is his opinion as to whether the military cuts in the Budget have not vastly increased the efficiency of the Defense Establishment?

Before however the General can even swallow, Mr. Pullman continues. He has only just returned from Washington—here he pauses and there is a murmur from the table —and he saw among many other officials, his good friend George Humphrey. At this Joe Lawler exclaims that he is the solidest man in the Government and there are general expressions of approval of Mr. Humphrey.

Mr. Pullman goes on. He does not wish to be quoted but George Humphrey has assured him that the country is in a healthy condition, and sound. And it will become even sounder in Mr. Pullman's opinion as the budget is balanced simultaneously with taxes being cut.

Mary Singer here intervenes and remarks that for her money, which she states it ultimately will be, she would rather have a lot more military power, and she deplores the cuts. And, she adds, she is sure that the General agrees with her.

Mr. Pullman looks surprised, and addresses Miss Singer as my dear young lady (showing that he is not aware of her identity). He tells her that it is a basic rule not to spend what you haven't got, and he for one is happy that at long last America is having a business Administration made up of men who understand that simple fact.

Miss Singer retorts that the Executive branch may be filled with businessmen, but there is after all Congress.

Ah Congress, Mr. Pullman replies, and looks a little depressed.

Furthermore, Miss Singer continues, if the country is so healthy and so sound, it can indeed afford the proper military posture for defense *and* attack; that it should be our over-riding policy to achieve this first priority, and she can only conclude from Mr. Pullman's remarks, that the country has not the money for this, because, and here she fixes Mr. Pullman with her eye, because we may very well be headed for a Recession!

Mr. Pullman gives a gasp, and Mrs. Bromley asks Mr. Lawler quite audibly who that woman is.

Mr. Pullman now reduces Mary Singer to my dear

Madam. We are, my dear Madam, he informs her, in a period of readjustment which is particularly healthy. We expect this year, based on total business activity, to be the highest in our history. If the backlog of orders is perhaps down, it is only one of the many signs that demand and supply are adjusting themselves to normal procedure.

Mrs. Bromley cries that this is wonderfully put, and doesn't the General agree.

Mary Singer, ignoring Mrs. Bromley, says, Look at the Farmers.

Mr. Pullman, his face quite rosy, cries that the farmers should beware of being led by radicals or they will be in serious trouble, eh General?

Mary Singer announces that the next election will show!

The *next* election! exclaims Mr. Pullman as one who is still licking his wounds from the last one.

Feel that at all costs must put an end to this interchange, and rescue the General from his position between the cross-fire, so spring to my feet and announce that everyone must help themselves to the next course.

The General propels me by my elbow to the buffet and I try to re-establish the mood of our earlier encounter at Nanking, but do not feel I am entirely successful. I see Mrs. Pullman maneuver herself next to her husband and give him a telegraphic message, at which he shows astonishment. But I have in the meantime maneuvered myself close to Charles and mutter my own directive which is for God's sake to serve up some champagne and cheer the party up, at which he shows even greater surprise than Mr. Pullman.

When I return to the table I find that Mr. Pullman has moved his seat and is next to Mary Singer, with his arm across the back of her chair in an atmosphere of marked intimacy. To say that his manner is fawning would be exaggerated, but words such as 'how absolutely right you are,' and 'that is a point that is well taken,' float over to me.

We all accordingly change places, and I find Mr. Case beside me. Mrs. Bromley sits next the General and I have a suspicion that they too may have met in Manila, only to hear them in a discussion of Deep Freezes, and which birds should be plucked, or frozen as are. The General is vivacious and Mrs. Bromley asks his advice on the correct gauge for woodcock. I realize that I have underestimated Mrs. Bromley.

As Mr. Case is the kind of conversationalist who allows one to continue one's own thoughts, I study Charles' table which has become so animated as to be called noisy, Estabrook Bromley's laugh causing the candles to shake and wax to fly in all directions.

Annie and Mrs. Biltz appear carrying bottles of champagne, and Major Sylvester suddenly rises, walks over to me, and murmurs that my husband wishes him to turn on the gramophone, and will I direct him as to where I have placed the dance records. Feel that Charles is under the misapprehension that the Major is now his Aide and start to apologize, when the General snaps his fingers at the Major, and says out of the corner of his mouth, Rumbas.

We all dance save Mr. Pullman and Mary Singer who remain absorbed in each other. Estabrook Bromley, like all heavy men, is extremely light on his feet, and Mr. Case, to the surprise of everyone, requests a tango for which we have no music. The General however is the master, and dances with incredible skill, changing partners punctiliously and never pausing for breath. He tells me that Dolly can do a very beautiful Hula which she learned when they were stationed in Hawaii, and I exclaim If only she would. Of course she will, declares the General, and then barks out, 'Major, Lovely Hands.' Did not know that I possessed this record, but it or its approximation sings softly through the room, as Dolly, introduced by Charles, throws off her little jacket, puts the orchid in her hair, and dances exquisitely with her pretty hands moving in and out as she circles around us.

There is thunderous applause and I pray to myself that this success will not inspire Beatrice Lawler to sing 'If You Knew Susie.' It does however, and it is a distinct anticlimax. The Major, sensing with Aide-like subtlety that this is enough of individual performances, now plays Liza, Embraceable You, and Here in My arms, and we all dance again.

At a certain moment the General, Dolly, and the Major, by some understood but unseen signal, all leave their partners and say good night. Dolly again remembers each name as she shakes hands, and again repeats her invitation that one and all are to come over and lunch with her at the Base.

Charles says to the General that he hopes his car is there, and the General and Major obviously feel that this is not even worthy of an answer. As I walk toward the door I think but am not sure that the Major, as he steps into the front seat of the low-slung khaki-colored Buick, next to a sergeant at the wheel, is carrying a record under his arm.

Shortly after this the others begin to take their leave. Mr. Pullman can hardly bear to tear himself away from Mary Singer and there is a last word to her that he hopes that she will read his address, made to the Retailers of America, which he will send to her. She might have missed it and he has had it printed for distribution among friends.

Mrs. Pullman invites us to a luncheon, and the Bromleys declare that they had once thought of buying in these parts but they can see it is far too gay. The Lawlers depart with that look of going on somewhere, and I try to explain to Mary Singer how the party grew and why, and we arrange to meet soon.

[31]

I go to search for Annie and find her cheek by jowl with Roza in the kitchen, both laughing loudly, which they immediately check when I enter, and which convinces me has been at my expense. Dear Maud and Hick drive Annie off between them, Annie clutching that little white envelope and looking slightly intoxicated.

Charles handsomely acknowledges that the party has been a success, but cannot understand why I ordered up all the champagne. Decide not to give him my real motivation but instead ask him if he does not now agree that it has been delightful to eat in the sitting room. Charles however reiterates that dining rooms are for dining.

May 22

Am extremely weary and call to the children from bed to get Daddy to take them to church. Daddy not around, so arrange by phone for lift, tell Rachel that Cissie can hold the contribution this time, and that they both must walk home, and on the left side of the road.

Rachel says she prefers going without me and would like to sit by herself in a pew, without Cissie, because it makes her feel more important. Too tired to deliver little homily on thoughts to be held in church.

Crawl downstairs, get some coffee and refuse to admit that a little dancing is what has done it; am touched to see that Charles has moved the furniture back into place without being asked. Find him outside with our neighbor Hick Tracy, who had driven over to discuss possibility of buying or renting mutual pick-up truck.

Make them sit down with me and rehash the dinner. Charles has found my friend Mary Singer attractive, and Hick declares that she certainly has something; therefore, they both demand, why has she never married? I say because she prefers to remain single.

All women want to marry, Hick declares.

It is all a woman ever thinks about, adds Charles.

If a woman does not marry, she feels herself a failure, continues Hick.

Miss Singer, I announce to them, is a highly successful lady at the top of her profession and the zenith of her career. I happen to know (which I don't) of at least six men who have been madly in love with her for years.

Then, says Hick, she is either secretly married to one of them, or is leading a sextuple life with all of them, or is vainly hoping that she still may trap one.

I declare that they are all vainly trying to trap her.

Never, never, exclaims Hick. I have never known a man who has not been hoodwinked into marriage. A woman is always the aggressor.

I give him an icy stare.

Charles now assumes a note of sweet reasonableness. A

woman, he informs me, would not be a womanly woman if she were otherwise. Because she is the guardian of the cradle of the race, in primeval fashion she knows that man's survival depends on her hunting instinct and animal cunning in ensnaring a mate. Only thus is she sure that the er-er tribe will increase.

Like Abou Ben Adhem? I inquire.

Hick says that Honey, you are so literary, the same as Miss Singer.

Find I am beginning to feel quite snappish. Men, I ask, are not interested in the future of the race?

Heavens no, says Charles. Men want to kill. They are just children.

Suggest rather peevishly to Charles that as it is Sunday he had better get the garbage out of the kitchen. Charles has however already done this which does not please me at all. Am quite ill-humored for several hours and only a nap after luncheon partially restores me.

Take Rachel on a walk with Old Joe and Taffy, Cissie refusing to leave her water coloring. The late afternoon is soft and glowing, the dogs bark about us, and I am suddenly filled with a sense of well-being. Suggest to Rachel we call on the two Miss Putnams who are after all neighbors.

Rachel says I must not call unless I invite them to something.

Would they enjoy coming for tea? No; Rachel believes they would like to be asked to a cocktail party.

I tell Rachel that we don't give cocktail parties in the country and what is more I don't believe either Miss Putnam would touch a drink. Rachel observes rather shrewdly that one never can tell, and anyhow what would make the two Miss Putnams happy would be to receive in the mail a card on which would be printed 'Won't you come to a cocktail party,' with two little cocktail glasses with cherries in them, in color, in one corner. She has seen these cards in the window of the drugstore. The Miss Putnams would then place this invitation on the mantel so everyone could see it.

I say to Rachel rather sharply that I think that kind of card is cheap. Rachel tells me there is a larger one that has roosters dancing a reel. I also add that it is shocking that a drugstore which makes up prescriptions, goes in for advertising liquor. Rachel remarks innocently that it is a wonderful drugstore; it has roller skates, paper backs, and electric irons. I adjure her not to mention any party to the Miss Putnams. I intend to invite them, but in my own good time.

Rachel then says she has to explain something to me that I may not quite understand. The Miss Putnams believe her name to be Pamela. I demand how that is possible, and Rachel is evasive but says she rather likes the name, so I am under no circumstances to call her 'Rachel,' or if I do accidentally, I am to cover it up by implying that it is a nickname.

I tell her that she was christened and so named after her dear great-aunt of which she should be proud, and Rachel replies softly that Oh yes she knows—Daddy's rich aunt, but anyhow I am not to give it away. Rachel looks so perturbed that I relent and tell her I will not call her anything, but that I find all this very deceitful.

The Miss Putnams are both in the back garden, the taller and I think older Miss Putnam spraying, while her sister directs. When the shorter Miss Putnam spies us, she gives a cry of pleasure and shouts at the taller Miss Putnam, who is apparently a little deaf, that Look, Look, it is Pam child and her mother, come to tell us about the ball!

Pamela, love! exclaims the taller Miss P. and we are enthusiastically led to the little porch.

I attempt to turn the conversation by admiring the shrubs, and ask the name of the insecticide, but the question is ignored. Both ladies have their eyes eagerly fastened on Rachel. I make a last valiant effort for truth and tell the Miss Putnams that Rach-er-Pamela must have been exaggerating. It was a Dinner. The Miss Putnams brush me aside. They want the affair described as seen through their Pammy's eyes.

Rachel has the grace to give me one furtive look,

and then plunges in. There were masses of flowers; many candles; much laughter; Champagne; and the music sounded throughout the house. (The gramophone.) The gowns were gorgeous—both ladies smile contentedly—and Mummy, who wore a sort of gold costume, had opened the Ball with the General, but Rachel herself had found a certain Major more glamorous.

The elder Miss Putnam says it must have looked like Waterloo.

The younger Miss P wants to hear more about the officers. Tell us about that Major, she pleads, don't be shy. And Louder, commands the elder Miss P.

Rachel gives a little smile and I jump up, make hasty apologies, and say I must get the dogs back.

Both ladies cry out in their disappointment. They tell me that Pammy is their sunbeam; they are two lonely old women and her visits are their greatest joy.

Rachel walks five feet ahead of me kicking stones as I attempt to explain to her (a) how wrong it is to be untruthful, (b) if she does not immediately mend her ways she will grow up a liar; and (c) how often does she visit the Miss Putnams? To (a) and (b) Rachel maintains she is not untruthful, she only exaggerates a little so that on (c) her visits to the Putnams, where she drops off from the school bus about twice a week, she can give them a good time.

Then Rachel adds pathetically that where we live now

she has not many friends close by; not even television. I tell her sternly to stop play-acting, and we march home.

(Will have to talk to Charles.)

May 24

Sister Julie telephones she is flying up on Wednesday by an airline she has discovered, which she is sure we do not know the existence of, and which lands at a Field that is in our general vicinity. Isn't that wonderful luck?

Charles figures on a map that this Field will take at least an hour and a half to reach by car, and that if Julie came the ordinary way by train it might lose her ten minutes, and save us about three hours and twenty minutes.

Julie however has to fly. She has not been in a train for six years, and her luggage and clothing are geared by weight.

Charles says he will meet her as it will give him an opportunity to investigate new Chinese laundry in neighboring town which might be able to do his seven Hong Kong shirts. These shirts, made for Charles while on a brief mission in Far East, are his dearest possession. Originally nine, one has been lost (everyone implicated in this), and one badly burnt by me and new steam iron, minus water.

This gives me my opportunity. I tell Charles that Chinese laundrymen are notorious for ripping shirts to rib-

bons; I would gladly drive the shirts over once a week—
Heavens, the forty minutes each way are nothing to me—
but what a risk. These Chinese might steal them, recognizing their quality. I have a better idea. Why not attempt
to get up from the city, Toona, former two-day-a-week
laundress, for say a couple of months? She might like the
country, and in between ministering to the shirts, she could
help with rooms, dishes, cleaning—I do not even have to
bring up the artillery. It is like taking candy from a child.
Charles' eyes gleam. He does not mention expense. He begs
me to write her immediately.

May 26

Dear Julie arrives, looking excessively smart but quite
gray in the face due to what she describes as 'one of the
roughest flights of my life.' The plane started late, and
dallied along the way. It was not pressurized, no steward
or stewardess, but a man in a sports jacket whose only sign
of officialdom was a cap with a black plastic visor, and who
had cried Whoops whenever there was a bump. The plane
had made five stops, and then had simply sat on the Field,
chatting with Piper Cubs.

Charles asks Julie why she did not take the train, and
Julie answers that she always flies.

May 27

The presents from Julie are an enormous success as she possesses the art of giving the flatteringly inappropriate.

Little Cissie receives a rakish hat which can be turned inside out in different color combinations, with *Suivez moi,* embroidered on one side, and *Je t'aime* on the other.

Charles is presented with a waistcoat of flowered silk which Julie tells him is The Thing now in London. (I rather regret this gift as can foresee immediate party to meet the waistcoat.) Rachel shrieks over a vanity case with 'Rachel' inscribed in bright stones, to which pale and dark lipsticks are linked, engraven *Midi* and *Minuit.*

Immediate argument ensues as to when and where a girl of thirteen may carry this case. Julie says of course to school for recess; Charles decrees Saturday nights at home; and I cruelly stipulate only when she calls on the Miss Putnams, at which Pamela gives me a baleful look.

Roza is bestowed a bottle of perfume, Lanvin Pretexte, and Julie tells her she must put a drop on each ear early in the morning, and then bring her up a cup of tea. Have never dared suggest a tray for myself in bed, but Roza seizes Julie's hand and kisses it. Julie then adds that she may have a dress or two for Roza to press after the jolts that plane gave her luggage. Roza appears delighted at this signal honor, rolls her eyes at the children and mutters to

Cissie that the Madame is a true Great Dane (Grande Dame?).

Julie now hands me what I assume is a brightly colored little shawl, and I immediately make two grave errors. I exclaim that this will be perfect for cold evenings, and I then hang it over my shoulders.

Julie screams at me in her Long Distance voice that I am wearing it like a shawl! She then snatches it from me, splits its thickness apart so it is half blue and half green, folds it into two triangles, and then slings it on with one corner tucked under, one side draped, an added twist which is inexplicable to me, and marches about in what appears to be a brand new costume.

I try again but cannot do it.

Charles now takes the shawl, folds it into its correct triangles, drapes it with a twist, looks like Molyneux, and is frightfully pleased with himself.

Julie adds to my confusion by showing another way to double it in two semicircles. Charles immediately masters this.

I say I am sure my trouble is that I am left-handed. Charles suggests that I take the waistcoat which he thinks with practice I could learn to button, and he will keep the shawl.

Julie admires the house, so wise of Charles to keep his uncle's old Victorian horror, and can already see that it is fraught with possibilities. My eyes stray to typewritten figures in wire basket, anticipate that by the time Julie is through with her fraughts at least five more pages will be added, and wish to change the subject.

Charles however becomes expansive under Julie's interest. Probably crazy not to have sold the old place, but he has reached that precise moment of his existence where he finds he wants something permanent. Of course when the book is done he will be back in harness, but he fully intends to spend as much of his life as he possibly can from now on out, in this old pile, gradually improving it of course, but make this Headquarters. Here Charles bangs the hearth and knocks over the tongs.

Julie nods and smiles, and Charles amplifies. It's good for a man to look out on a few acres of his own. There comes a time when one should root in, narrow the horizon, Belong. Charles is happy to say he has, at long last, reached that point.

Julie breaks into applause and says she is sure he is running for Congress. Charles looks a little discouraged, and asks how soon Brink, Julie's husband, is arriving.

Brink it appears is already flying 'the other way' across the Aleutians to Northern Alberta, there to investigate and assess the possibilities of oil. Julie will join him when he has found a place to live. Am stunned by this. Julie does not know length of assignment. Says she prays now every night that man will stop advancing frontiers. If only oil could be discovered in the sewers of Paris. Saudi Arabia had the climate of a furnace, and the sand was always in her eyes, but at least in a day she could be in Cairo or Istanbul—remind her to tell us about the island in the Sea of Marmora where someday she and Brink will live—but in Alberta it will be forty below—still it may be fun; Eskimo girl friends but hopeful she will be the only white woman. . . .

The more Julie goes on, the more jealous I become, and the more my foot itches. Julie and I sit up late, and I notice as the room grows chilly she takes my new shawl and puts it on absentmindedly and in a most conventional manner.

Find Charles stretched out on his bed staring at ceiling. He says that it sounds crazy, but honestly he would like to quit book, fireside, wife, children, and while he still has his faculties, go on one hell of a trip.

JUNE

June 1

Julie possesses two hobbies which move with her wherever she travels, involve practically no equipment or air weight, and supply her with never-ending resource.

The first is letter writing and letter receiving. Some part of each day Julie goes to her room 'to attend to my desk.' From a host's point of view this is ideal behavior for if there is no entertainment afoot Julie appears to welcome extra time for vast world-wide correspondence.

Julie writes to blood relatives or chance friends with equal fervor. She is faithful beyond death and I believe continues epistles to bereaved whom she may never have seen. She does not believe in tooth for tooth communications but writes, indifferent to response. Invariably and eventually receives replies and thus no friendships wither from neglect (as mine do), but bloom forever in her garden.

Julie's mail resembles that of United Nations Official, and she likes to share contents with whoever is near. Thus this morning little Cissie in informed that André is in trouble again because of Gogo, poor dear, and Charles is given the news that that nice French Colonel Lambert has been transferred to Rabat which is a step down.

Always too productive to ask Julie who Gogo and Lambert are, so Charles gives a kind of yes-no grunt, acquired over the years in listening to these fragments.

It is when Julie suddenly opens up with second hobby that my heart sinks. Julie believes herself to be not only a Decorator but an Architect. Having moved frequently in her life from hacienda to run-down palazzo, to hermitage, to mansion, she has invariably redone and left her stamp. If luxurious she simplifies, if pastoral she introduces the metropolitan note. Her guiding principle is to transform, but she has always wrought these mutations in lands that apparently abound in willing handy-crafty slave labor and what she calls 'little men who help me.'

Julie satisfies this hobby when nothing of her own is at hand by suggesting innovations in the homes of her friends and relatives. Where once complacency reigned over pretty wallpapers and painted furniture, Julie sows her dragon's teeth and a great crop of dissatisfaction flourishes.

Julie opens up on me rather gently. She thinks it is wonderful that at last I have an opportunity to do what I want, and express my own sense of elegance which she has always believed that latently I possess but so far have never revealed.

I decide to take a stand very early in this bout, and declare that children and elegance are unhappy partners, and that dollars, not lire or pesetas, are going to govern what we do.

Julie shrugs this off. We will talk about that after we decide on the over-all scheme. I say I have a limited scheme, and so has Charles. Julie is courteous but not very interested because she already has the Grand Design.

She then announces one of her dictums. A Victorian house can either be amusing, or distinguished. Amusing is already old hat and out because even department stores have taken it up. Therefore that leaves Distinguished, and here Julie gives a sigh which implies that this will be quite beyond me.

Having let this little wasp out of her box, she moves on. Thank God the house has high ceilings. And potential space. But neither height nor space are used to their full advantages. They must be emphasized. Julie now gives her second dictum. There is nothing like Knocking Down Walls.

Tell her proudly that I also want to knock down a wall, and show her small hall next little back room. Julie says this is chicken feed and proves nothing. No, as she sees it, and here she half closes her eyes as though gazing on the Pyramids, she would begin by knocking down entire wall between large living room and big hall, and then, then, get four marble columns (Doric or Corinthian) and stand them in place of old wall. This will be dramatic and give focus.

Ask her rather sharply where she thinks I will find marble columns even if I so wished. Julie says I should jump in the car, explore, and discover some nice abandoned, old Greek Revival house, saw off its wooden columns, and stick them up. After all the fun of fixing a place is to make-do.

See the lines of battle beginning to be drawn and now wish Charles was with me, but it is sacred time for writing so have to fend for myself. Tell Julie my only desire is to have a practical house that will work. Julie replies that she has never seen columns that did not work. I explain what I mean by practical. Julie responds Oh you mean functional, why didn't you say so?

I cry out that all I want in this world is a beautiful kitchen with Equipment as I spend a lot of time there, on and off; that I think Doric columns are frightfully old hat and look like movie theaters of the twenties.

Think this shaft goes home. Interruption from Cissie bringing me special delivery letter and see from penciled address on envelope that it is from Toona. I rip it open, breathing heavily, and hope Julie will think it is from my lover.

Toona writes she will try it, no cooking, but can she bring along Gregory, her son, who nice boy, clean.

Julie inquires anxiously if something has happened. I say No, no . . . not really, but I have to leave her now . . . to think something out. Thus achieve brief respite from advice on alteration.

Must talk to Charles and try to put backbone into him against next onslaught.

June 4

Charles urges that we include Gregory (son of Toona, the two-day laundress) 'if he is the right age.' As have never known of his existence, ask Charles how old in his opinion he should be? Charles suggests about fourteen which I tell him I would not like at all. Charles adds that he could clean shoes and roll tennis court. This is so fanciful that I write Toona suggesting that she came up for a couple of weeks alone and try it, and then we can talk about Gregory.

THE DINNER PARTY

Invite Julie to go to PTA meeting with me and Julie says she does not know what I am talking about, and when I explain, she replies God forbid, she wants to wash her hair and 'brood' about the house.

PTA meeting quite successful but should have worn hat. Miss Licks thinks Rachel is a good little student. She will however need tutoring this summer in mathematics as coming from another school, she is behind. Would think numbers would add and subtract the same from coast to coast but naturally do not dare say this.

Cissie I am told is a dear child but sensitive. Am not sure if this is a compliment. Long discussion concerning girls spying on boys when they strip for gymnasium (little window at top of wall in hall to be covered with beaverboard), the craze of card trading to be discouraged at home as well as at school; and how do we mothers feel about Tuesday afternoon activities.

I make strong plea for plain cooking for all sons and daughters, instead of ceramics and toreutics, which I find means metal work. Am slapped down hard and told that Home Economics comes in tenth grade. What is now being discussed is Art.

Due to my unfortunate suggestion, am later unanimously elected chairman of Cake Counter at coming School Fair. Can see have deceived fellow mothers into believing that I majored in Domestic Science, and therefore will never be invited to be a judge of paintings or essays which I should enjoy.

Three fathers attend meeting which I must not forget to mention to Charles. Mr. Parsons, who several ladies whisper to me is a 'recent' widower, I discover is partner in firm which has sent in bid on our alteration. Think it would be incorrect to mention this over orangeade and gingersnaps, but Mr. Parsons brings it up. Hopes we can get started before plasterers leave on Wherry Housing job at Army Base.

Tell him estimate appears a little high and we will have to shave it down. (Why don't I say it is enormous and we must cut out a lot?)

Mr. Parsons says just so we get started. I reply Yes indeed, and give smile, as it is social occasion. Sense other women believe I am trying to lay trap for widower. Finally get away and Mr. Parsons calls after me that he hopes he will hear from me. Do not answer.

June 5

Long airmail letter arrives from friend entrusted with project of finding correct name of little Louise's parents, so that I can extend invitation for visit which Louise has already written Cissie she intends to make.

Friend writes that Louise's parents are divorced and both

remarried—isn't that sad. Read letter to Charles and Julie, and Julie and I agree that generally remarriages make for happiness and that the 'isn't that sad' note is a cliché.

I analyze letter further and inform Julie that by its contents I can deduce when the divorce took place. It was, I conclude, three years ago because during the first two years all parties concerned fight for possession of 'The Child' as the 'isn't that sad' school call her, but after three years the struggle concerns itself with getting rid of Child by frequent visits in holidays so that the new alignments can be free. Louise now knows what Maisie knew.

Charles says he hates my cynicism and rather ostentatiously opens dark brown book which he gazes at with his back toward us. This delights Julie who asks in a deep-throated whisper if I have not observed that the childless couples are the real lovers, as the woman is not split in her allegiance in thirds, quarters, or sevenths.

I reply indeed I have noticed almost every hour on the hour, whereupon Charles, still with his back toward us, comments that we are apparently unaware that the only purpose of marriage is race survival, not story-book love, at which Julie protests and Charles turns another page.

Julie now manipulates conversation with me so that she and I, and a rather select group, are hanging onto small raft in the Pacific, faced with some hard choices as to who we push up onto raft so that Race can survive. There is, Julie adds as an afterthought, a tidal wave and it is the end of the world.

I suggest we save one man and two women. Julie agrees a bit reluctantly, but says she sees my point. What types shall they be? I nominate a brain woman and a brawn woman, but we are undecided if the man shall be brain or brawn. Julie declares that Charles would be an ideal type as he combines both features, don't I think? Charles however is not mollified.

Julie now casts her line in another direction. After about fifteen years of Charles and brain-woman and brawn-woman, living idyllically together on Atoll with their dozens of beautiful children, brain-woman hears there is one survivor from way out yonder whom she wants to secure as a son-in-law. What race shall he belong to?

Charles cannot resist this fly and snaps at it. My son-in-law, he states in a sepulchral voice, must be an Englishman. Julie and I are equally astounded.

At this moment there is a roll of thunder and all the lights in house go out. I give a shriek and feel someone has walked over my grave. Rush upstairs and find Cissie and Rachel happily watching storm at open window, with Taffy under the bed and Old Joe cowering in corner. Bring all down and we light candles and listen to the rain. Much later at night give a second scream when all lights suddenly go on again. Charles gallantly gets up and turns off switches and I sleep again, uneasily dreaming of an atoll.

June 8

Come to grips with Julie and Charles on alteration in three-handed bout, where I squat like Clara between the pacing Mr. and Miss Murdstone. Julie I sense has already penetrated a few of Charles' defenses, and each holds yellow pad, Julie's covered with writing and diagrams, and Charles' a blank.

Julie nominates and elects herself chairman, and moves in briskly with the opening remarks. Of course it is our house, and in the end obviously we must do what we want. She will alas not be here to see our innovations, but she would not feel right with herself before she leaves, if she did not make two small points.

(a) Eliminate, eliminate, eliminate.

Tell her this is standard medical advice, and Julie says hush or I will break the thread, which I am only too anxious to do.

(b) Starting with bedrooms, eliminate half the closets (or cupboards as she calls them rather affectedly) and substitute wide open shelves so that 'I can see what I have.'

Tell her I know only too well, but am hushed again.

(c) Passing reference to need of eliminating all box

springs on beds as bad for back and carriage. Arabs stand erect because they sleep on rug on ground.

(d) Eliminate all curlicues on banisters. Little carpenter can do this in ten minutes.

(e) Eliminate worn turkey-red stair carpet and wax, wax, wax stair treads until they are so shiny and slippery that a child might break its leg. This is the traditional French method of confirmation of proper polish. (Brief digression here on bare floors—beautiful; carpets—vulgar; and rugs, small and valuable, or eliminate.)

Julie now announces that so far she has spent about twenty dollars and already a teeny bit of style, like one beam of sunlight, is creeping in. She continues from pad.

(f) Eliminate large stained glass multi-paned window on stair landing (which makes her want to throw up every time that she sees faces turn green or salmon as they pass) and install wider curved window.

I make sentimental plea that the children love the colored panes, and Charles makes stronger statement that nothing costs as much as curved glass.

Julie clears her throat and continues. We are now at the rez-de-chaussée and this is the salient of the house. And what do we find? Here she pauses and shudders.

With wide doors which when open expose room after room, there is no Rest for the Eye but a clash in chromism of blue, red, or what have you, in peeling wallpapers, carpets, love seats covered in wrong color silk, smudgy old portraits of anybody's ancestors, and, so help her, two Japanese fans thumb-tacked up over an imitation ivory elephant.

Hotly explain that fans were given to me by Cissie for my birthday, and that I am devoted to elephant and that he *is* ivory.

Charles makes single notation on his pad—'elephant' with a question mark.

Julie perseveres. We have fine cornices and some surprisingly good marble mantels. Therefore, cries Julie, we must go Off-White throughout. We must Be Italian.

Charles puts down pad and says Thanks a lot, your suggestions are marvelous and we shall certainly think about them, but unfortunately first things come first i.e. new oil burner. Julie however maintains her course. She asks Charles price of burner and he, falling into what I can see is an ambush, names an outrageous figure.

Exactly, cries Julie, for a third of that you could have a man, in one of those nice, striped cotton jackets, living in the house and keeping open fires roaring all winter, plus stoking old coal furnace which was good enough for the ancestors, plus waxing the floors, plus a little valeting on the side.

Perceive only too clearly that Charles' ears are pricking, and Julie quickly presses her advantage. Charles has always been to her a man who stood not only for truth but for beauty. Is he now becoming the standard American who falls in love with an oil burner and wants to show off his thermostat instead of his Guardi?

She then concludes, divining that if victory is not yet snatched, she has scattered enough confusion to consolidate when she chooses.

> Eliminate
> Paint off-white throughout
> Wax
> Knock down long wall

Privately thank my stars that Julie has forgotten the kitchen.

June 9

Luncheon at Pullmans' to which we take Julie. Explain Pullmans so she can decide what to wear. Julie says she always wears what she feels like wearing, but agrees after my description it is more subtle to underdress.

She then gives new dictum. If no hat, wear gloves. Gloves and shoes may match, or gloves and belt may match, but Never all three. Gloves and shoes may be brown, or rust, but Never match bright colors.

I say, Obviously, in a worldly way, and then run upstairs

and dig out from chest in very dark 'cupboard' three pair of white cotton, one pair of brown kid (black at finger-tips) and three single lefts of the right shade. Go into Linda's room and find in her bureau expensive English chamois gloves which I gave her for Christmas, and still in their cellophane wrapping. Feel like Indian Giver, but take them.

Day is rainy and cold and contemplate new shawl over dress but cannot imagine how I will manage my arms freely during lunch, so discard idea. Wear tweed suit and Charles shines shoes for me.

Julie adds five exquisite Roman gold bracelets to her gloves. Hide my leather wristwatch under my sleeve. Charles takes the longest to get ready, and then comes down in normal gray flannels and jacket. (What do men Do when they dress?)

Delay in starting as Old Joe will not get out of car because of rain and when he is pulled out Taffy jumps in bringing mud onto seat. As we take off Rachel says, Oh, you have swiped Linda's new gloves, but do not think Julie hears.

Pullmans have long drive with macadam surface which we all agree is a strike against them, but Charles regretfully remarks that the trees are very fine. Many cars in large blue gravel turn-around, one with a District of Columbia license which I point out.

Hostile butler opens door with overtone that we are late which is after all impossible at a week-end luncheon. Shown into large room and am greeted effusively by our now apparently intimate friends, the Estabrook Bromleys. Mrs. Pullman is wearing a hat and Mrs. Bromley is not, which confuses Julie as to who is hostess. Do not know other guests who appear frighteningly smart and up to date, though am happy to perceive that Julie must be having same effect on the ladies as she shakes hands about the room. Do not know why normal gesture of shaking hands causes so many women such acute embarrassment, but can detect that Julie's leisurely manner of doing so is nettling to them, and delightful to the men where her pace becomes more lingering.

The men divide fairly evenly into two categories; those of the healthy, sporting executive mold, and those belonging to the fagged Government administrator caste. (Possibly reach this last conclusion because of D.C. automobile plate out front.) Mr. Pullman therefore appears today as a split personality. He is still rosy, and he wears a checked bowtie, but his eyes look a little anxious, and he does not have the same bounce. Cannot imagine what has occurred in the last two weeks to bring about this change.

Mr. Pullman tells me that I am to be seated next to a very important man, probably the most important now Behind the Scenes. Am thrilled. Ask his name but at that

moment antagonistic butler approaches and informs **Mr.**
Pullman, a little more loudly than necessary, that Washington is On the Phone. Mr. Pullman rushes out and I **am**
alone with butler. Butler asks me if I would like another
cocktail, and I tell him tartly I have not yet had one. He
gives me a sardonic look and glides away and I am left **by**
myself at the piano. It is covered with enormous silver
and leather-framed pictures. In the exact center is President Eisenhower, autographed. Directly behind are **Queen**
Marie of Roumania and Herbert Hoover. To the left **are**
Bernard Baruch, sitting, Earl Warren, and Admiral Rad-
ford. To the right are Calvin Coolidge, a group picture of
Firestone, Edison and Ford, and Adolphe Menjou.

Mrs. Pullman appears by my side and I compliment **her**
on so interesting a collection. Mrs. Pullman answers **that**
there is nothing like a grand piano for showing off photo-
graphs. (Wonder if Steinway & Sons would appreciate **this**
tribute.)

Olivia, the daughter, now joins us, and Mrs. Pullman,
who I perceive is becoming agitated by telephone call **now**
going on full blast—surely Mr. P. must have library **where**
he could talk more privately—hastily says, You know **my**
Olivia, and flies out to hall just as both Olivia and I dis-
tinctly hear Mr. Pullman exclaim: God damn it, Lucius
Clay told me the exact opposite!

Cannot imagine what this momentous conversation is

about but am convinced that I am indeed quite fortuitously overhearing some debate on Government policy. Only wish Charles were beside me as he would undoubtedly understand what General Clay had asserted that now appears to be raising so much dust.

Olivia, looking very bored for a girl of sixteen, remarks that Well, it's come at last; poor Pa hasn't left the house for two weeks waiting for the phone to ring.

Do not know what response to make to this, but before I can even begin to evolve one, Mr. Pullman, voice now near the cracking point, cries out: I am not interested in the Dominican Republic, and you can tell Sherman Adams to go to Hell!

Fortunately most of the guests are at the other end of the room. Ask Olivia if she does not think we should close the door, but she replies, quite accurately, that with Pa that does no good. She then says that it's all so Tahsome—surely an odd comment—and gives me a languid look. (Think Olivia shaves her eyebrows.)

Mr. Pullman however is again speaking and his tone though glacial, has a hint of melt in it.

. . . It is disheartening to be regarded as a fund-raising wheelhorse. . . . Reward for Texas? Fantastic! Even the press can't sell him. . . . No, he won't last. . . . With the Boss! Well, that's damn decent of you, Ed. . . . right . . . Tuesday, if you can arrange it . . . right . . . appointment to be confirmed . . . right . . . meet you first at the Mayflower . . . right . . . right . . .

Mrs. Pullman is the first to re-enter the room, her face now wreathed in smiles. Mr. Pullman follows, writing in a small leather book which he places in an inner pocket. The butler tells the room that we are going to have something to eat, and we cross the hall like a flock of sheep, in search of a better grazing ground.

The table is long and is decorated with a very wide mirror down its center. This has the curious consequence of giving an unvarnished panorama of the nostrils and upper teeth of the eight people sitting along the opposite side of the table. (Must ask Julie if this is Italian.)

Charles is placed on Mrs. Pullman's right at which I am flattered. Wish though that he did not eat with such transparent relish. Do not know why company food is so superior in everyone else's house, and why everyone but me can produce a consistent meal of novelties that are delicious. Would never have occurred to me to put mushrooms under finger bowls and have so many treasures hidden in a mold of aspic. Decide to toy with my food to counteract the obvious starvation of Charles.

One of the two men I am sitting next is, I have been told, the most important now Behind the Scenes, but do not know which one. Must find out, so consider swiftly what shall be my first shot. There is no particular clue from their

[61]

appearance. Left Side is bald, Right Side has a mustache, both look tired, and neither is wearing week-end sports clothes. Fortunately the table has not yet firmed up into Noah's Ark prototype and there is still time for a three-handed warm-up. (Must conceal I am a Democrat, but slide in that Charles is a Republican.)

Open with practice serve. Ask if either of you gentlemen own the car in the drive with the Washington license plate? Am asked in return if I am thinking of buying a new automobile because if so— Have made a fault and so quickly send another ball which just gets over the net. No, I mentioned car because I am so interested in meeting anyone who has just left Washington.

A lot more will be leaving than will ever get there, says Bald-Man, and Mustache-Man roars with laughter. Bonhomie thus unwittingly established, and we all take off our sweaters.

Mustache now seizes the initiative and sends to my backhand by asking me What I do. (Always an unfair question as know that am overworked, but invariably find it impossible to explain How to any man.) Reply obliquely that my husband is at home all day as he is doing a book.

This causes usual looks of apprehension from both Bald and Mustache, so hastily add that of course he isn't a real writer, he is just writing a book. (Feel this could be better expressed, sounds disloyal, and am quite unhappy.)

Mustache asks me to point my husband out, which I do, and as an afterthought give his name, at which Bald exclaims, Of course, I know all about him, and then adds in the most meaningful way to Mustache, He is going to be Used.

Am so excited by this significant observation, which has been entirely voluntary, that for a moment I cannot speak. Is this not tantamount to broad hint that as Mr. Pullman has refused Dominican Republic, Charles will be offered it, and should it not be a ten times bigger post as Charles is fifty times cleverer than Mr. P?

Realize that I must proceed with utmost caution, so merely throw out as casually as I can that God knows They have been after him. (Wonder if this is a little strong?)

That's funny, says Bald, as I clear for this area.

Do not quite like the trend of this comment as am pretty sure that Ambassadors are not appointed by area, and have disquieting thought that Bald, who I now fully recognize as Man Behind the Scenes, may be slating Charles for quite another type of post. Think quickly as to how to handle this and finally say very thoughtfully, in a deliberative sort of way, that of course Charles is fundamentally a Diplomat.

He'll need strong-arm methods here all right, all right, says Bald, if we're going to keep this district in the column. Hope that Hubby of yours is a good money-raiser.

Am so outraged that this horrible little man should think of Charles in terms of fund-raising for a Congressional District that am for several seconds speechless. As I am planning the most insulting rejoinder I can possibly produce, the table goes through a tidal shift and Bald and Mustache both turn away from me, having won the first set, and I am left crumbling a roll on the sidelines.

As I am seated in dead center at the side of table, there is no possibility of catching on anywhere with vague, appreciative laughter. Difficult to look alert when you cannot distinguish what anyone is saying, so concentrate on Waldorf salad (rather rich) and Virginia ham. Butler comes up behind me and blows some words down my neck which sound like 'mutton Rothschild, forty-seven.' Do not understand what he is saying, so he decodes in low but condescending voice: Red Wine, Madam. Wave him away and feel humiliated.

Consider as dispassionately as I can what my companions at luncheon have told me, and try to analyze what the real import of their remarks is. Then one of those flashes supposed to emanate from Jove, blinds and then illuminates me. As an election is already casting its long shadow, have I not quite accidentally been given forewarning that if this area is vital to Republican hopes, it must ipso facto be equally so to aspirations of the Opposition? Have I not an obligation to dig out any evidence I stumble upon from

Man Behind the Scenes of future political schemes, and then pass on to my side?

Dessert is now making the rounds, a great globe of chocolate and whipped cream, in stripes, and as Bald turns to scoop into it, I grab him. Tell him I am disturbed by his hint that there is trouble anticipated in these parts (false), and would like to know what his plans are (true).

Bald, surprised by my sympathetic interest, jumps in. Gives me what he calls over-all picture of general situation which is good, in fact excellent. A few soft spots here and there, but reports are optimistic.

Unfortunately, and here Bald lowers his voice, due to sudden demise of Congressman L., there will have to be special election early in the autumn for successor to fill out term. As there has always been a Republican Congressman representing us as far back as he can remember, it would be very, very serious if for some inexplicable reason there was an upset.

Nearly fall into his whipped cream from excitement but keep my voice even and inquire why he envisages such a possibility.

Because, says Bald, sometimes an electorate is unaccountable. Because there is always danger in a bi-election. It is a pity that Congressman L. passed over, it is in fact bad luck, for though he never did anything, he was taken for granted, and was a Fixture. When you have a Fixture who is a Fixture in the true sense of the word, at least 9 per cent of the voters know his name, and you are safe.

In normal times continues Bald, one can ask what does one Congressional election matter more or less? But the new and disquieting element is the attitude of some of the newspapers which have recently been getting way out of line. If for any reason—and one must always in politics recognize such a possibility—this election went Democratic, the press might interpret it as a Trend. Nothing in Bald's opinion would be worse for the Party than even a hint of a Trend, anywhere at all. Trends can be forest fires unless handled.

See Mrs. Pullman preparing to rise, so hastily ask who will be candidates.

Party leaders will select ablest man available, replies Bald, and then, lowering his voice, he gives me the nugget. He hopes the Democrats do not choose a *Veteran.*

Chairs scrape and Mrs. Pullman leads the ladies out while the men remain with Mr. P. in dining room. (Preposterous to separate at luncheon party and am sure by now everyone like myself wants to get home.)

Weather has turned into Scotch mist and Mrs. P. tells us it is far too wet to see her spring flowers. She then makes the statement to which I have never been able to evolve appropriate response: I am a passionate gardener.

Sit in semicircle in a kind of stupor, aftermath of enor-

mous lunch, and a series of topics are dealt with, ranging
from King Farouk, June train schedules, Clare Boothe
Luce—beautiful of course but to a Latin country is it wise
—the new book by what's his name, I never can think of
the title, and best poison ivy cream.

Walk over to French windows with Julie and see Charles
pacing up and down terrace with several men, including
Bald. Disturbed by sight. Mrs. Bromley joins us and asks
how 'our' dear General is. He is not Mrs. Bromley's general at all.

Men finally appear and Julie causes terrific flap by announcing she is going to walk home. Everyone offers lifts
and no one will believe her when she says that she likes to
walk. Consternation from Estabrook Bromley and Mr.
Pullman when they learn she plans to cut across country.
Mr. P. goes to Charles with grave face and says she may
get lost. Julie suggests she then could ask the way. Mr.
P. declares there are even 'cattle' about. Julie boldly states
she is not frightened.

By this time most of us are out on the gravel turn-
around to watch her take-off. Mr. Pullman attempts to
chart her course, and advises bearing south by south-
west which I know only too well can mean nothing to a
woman.

Suddenly charming young man whom I had not particularly observed before seizes Julie's hand, pushes her into

front seat of car and goes off with her with pleased smile on his face. Car has District of Columbia license plate.

On drive home decide I must explain to Charles my rather dubious behavior as Trojan horse. Charles listens patiently, with frequent yawns, and then asks why I went to such elaborate lengths to discover somthing that has been in the papers for a week—namely, that a bi-election is coming up which both Parties will try to win.

Feel a little flattened by this.

Charles says he has a serious problem and he needs my best advice. When he gets home, shall he take a nap, or take a walk? Suggest he play croquet with children and Charles responds that he thinks he will take a nap.

Ask him if he knows name of man who kidnaped Julie, and Charles replies George Pullman told him that he is the most important man now behind the scenes.

Charles plays croquet with Rachel and Cissie, and I fall into a sodden slumber. Julie does not return until nearly midnight, discloses nothing beyond the fact that she had a beautiful walk, and assures Charles that she did not get her feet wet.

June 10

As it is the day of Julie's departure Charles and I both decide to take her to airport. Julie announces that this time she is not going to fly, she simply will not put us to all that trouble. Charles, quite touched at this awareness on her part, brings out new train schedules, and Julie looking a little evasive, says a friend has kindly offered to drive her to the city.

D.C. license appears, and charming young man's name is disclosed as Bill Dighton, though Charles apparently hears it as Pearson and the matter is never quite cleared up. Dighton-Pearson helps carry the bags out, and Roza presents Julie with bouquet, having cut my only five roses which have bloomed, and hospitably urges her to come back soon for longer visit as it will be very dull up here on the hill without her.

Julie gazes at leaden sky and says Isn't it a *divine* day, and she and Dighton-Pearson both laugh. Feel quite old. She then embraces Charles and says that when she returns, she wants him to read every line of his book out loud to her, and implores him not to disappoint me on all those wonderful changes that I so crave for the house.

Cissie, who has climbed into car suddenly wails out: But where are you going? to which Dighton-Pearson replies, Very far I hope. Rachel, looking quite perturbed, says loudly, Give my love to Uncle Brink.

They finally drive off and leave us feeling quite flat. The truth of the Spanish saying is borne in on me 'The Road is always better than the Inn.'

Tell children to get ready for church and usual argument ensues over temperature, jackets, and sandals versus shoes.

Sit on bottom step, with Charles above me rereading yesterday's paper, and we discuss Julie. Ask how he thinks the little trip will end, and he replies that he is sure of one thing only, that Julie will write letters to the man from Washington for the rest of her days, and then read the replies out loud to Brink.

Ask if he would mind if I went off on similar jaunt so merrily, and he answers that I should know by this time that the you-and-me brand of examination is apt to end in blows or wounds. If he says I would mind, I will accuse him of insularity, and if he says I would not mind, I will charge him with indifference.

Tell him I think I would prefer it if he minded, and Charles, with a loud sigh, asks if I do not think that one of the beauties of having been married as long as we have is that we do not have to be so personal about it any more. Am astounded by this interpretation of the beauty of marriage. Deliver short speech on that relationship which I assure Charles can only be kept alive and significant if never taken for granted. Charles says that sounds awfully fatiguing and what is so wrong about taking it for granted —wouldn't it be rather jumpy not to?

Say that a woman likes to be confident about herself.

and if she does not get this very personal reassurance from her husband, she may hunt for it elsewhere. Charles asks why I'm getting the wind up and pats me on the top of head with rolled-up newspaper.

Point out that the reason Julie appears so buoyantly youthful is that her marriage has never grown stodgy. Charles tells me that in the early morning I honestly look younger than she. Make mistake of inquiring about the evening and he replied that of course then she absolutely knocks your eyes out.

(Find this cold comfort, as who sees my buoyant youth in early morning? Recall the many French novels where man and woman, or even husband and wife, have long intricate toi-et-moi dialogues analyzing their emotional susceptibilities, and then often follow it with letters to each other, written only a few hours later, restating the enigma of their passion. Am aware however that this probably too much to demand of Charles.)

Rachel and Cissie appear—in sandals—and Rachel asks if we do not think Aunt Julie and that man who kept smiling so foolishly looked like a scene in the movies when they drove off? Charles answers that she might as well learn it early—life Is like the movies—and on this note I take children to church.

As feel I have been a little petulant in conversation with Charles, plan to discipline myself by playing demoralizing game whereby I will assume that any admonition or counsel appearing in sermon, is particularly directed at me from On High. Recognize that this is more the approach to Medium or Oracle than to Guidance, but have over many years tapped wood, avoided cracks, and left-shouldered the moon and have received a strange comfort from my superstitions.

Church is crowded and had forgotten Bishop to be present. Cissie in ecstasy over canticle and joins loudly to praise Him, and magnify Him forever, as the Sun and Moon, Floods, Snow, Whales and Fowls of the air, bless the Lord. Even Rachel has not the heart to frown at her. Sermon is on Charity (for Missions) and am committed to apply its immediate lesson, so take little envelope which children shove at me, and fill in my name for larger amount than I normally might have done.

Linger outside and try to enlist possible contributors for School Fair, which should have done a week ago. Feel that I am regarded as slightly commercial on a Sunday but cannot see why this is not more worthy than an engagement made for golf which I overhear.

Maud, who rarely goes to church, asks me if I am Doing Anything about the Bishop. This has not occurred to me but immediately feel guilty, and give half-hearted invitation to tea. Nice Rev. Perkins says alas, he is driving Bishop to neighboring parish. Immediately become very hos-

pitable and am sure even children sense my hypocrisy. Tell
Maud rather severely that if she has such a conscience for
obligations (of others) will she contribute two cakes to my
table? Maud promises, and says she may even make them
herself, which I impore her not to do.

In afternoon it showers again and Rachel and I get
Toona's room ready. Charles gives Cissie ping-pong lesson and then announces that we are taking dogs on long
walk, rain or no rain.

Violets are gone and apple blossoms over, but lilacs are
still blooming and I steal an armful from deserted farm on
higher hill. Nothing in this world has the rapture of the
scent of wet lilacs, and branches that are stolen smell
sweetest.

June 13

Drive five miles to meet Toona. Decide not to mention
son Gregory to her for a few days till I see which way the
wind is blowing.

Can find Toona nowhere among passengers. Run up
and down platform and just as I am giving up she emerges
from front coach and says she did not know this was a
station. Toona carries two paper bags and one small straw
valise. Ask her if that is all her luggage and she rolls her
eyes and says Oh yes.

We get into car and I tell her she looks fine (meaning strong), and Toona replies that city in summer always agrees with her. She then adds she did not know we lived so far away, which is palpably ridiculous as sent two letters with directions, plus timetable.

Have never in past had much conversation with Toona as always in basement laundry in apartment house, but point out two lakes, the higher hills, and panoramic view. Toona asks where the houses are, so I change to news of children and pleasure of Charles at her arrival. Give over-humorous description of Hong Kong Shirts to which she does not particularly respond, but finally volunteers that it looks like it rains here.

Rachel and Cissie outside with dogs when I bear her in on my shield. Cissie kisses her while Old Joe barks joyfully and can see that Toona is pleased. Take her back to the kitchen and Roza says, Well I never thought they would get You up here. Ask Roza if she will show her room, and then flee, as cannot think exactly how to begin. (This procrastination on my part is serious as should know exactly what I expect of Toona and tell her clearly, but have sometimes had the luck to have services proffered which I have lacked the imagination and courage to suggest.)

Maud comes over in afternoon and I give her description of delightful tea party I held for Bishop on Sunday, and my gratification at his praise of my good works.

Maud asks if I want a red-hot idea for my good works i.e. the cake sale. I tell her indeed I do, that I need all of the help I can get. Maud outlines proposal. She will install small tent directly behind my stall, disguise herself as an Egyptian 'or something like that,' and tell Fortunes by means of Crystal Ball. Anyone spending more than two dollars at my booth will receive a reading gratis, or may buy one direct, and profits will be chalked up to my table.

Can see this is brilliant but ask Maud what makes her believe she can be a soothsayer? What does she know about it?

Maud says to have no fear as on visit to San Francisco she watched friend, regarded on Pacific coast as Oracle. Friend became celebrity after allegedly ruining a man by perceiving in crystal ball that market was going up when it actually went down. Maud acquired technique from this seeress, and enumerates for me various tricks of trade she has mastered.

As men more superstitious than women, generally preferable to do them with dirty pack of cards stacked with Black Ladies; for unknown clients assume they are all misunderstood, hope to meet 'a stranger' and must beware, and then ring the changes on letters to come, pots of gold, journeys, and a little trouble which can however be weathered.

This however says Maud is easy and innocent. The

cream of the jest will lie in the artful handling of friends and acquaintances. Who therefore do I think is likely to appear at my table?

I tell her that anyone who makes donation to a Fair always hangs around watching to see if it sells. Get list and read out: 'Contributions to date for my Concession. Mr. Case—promised 2 doz. Brownies; Mrs. Pullman—generous but vague; the Misses Putnam—doughnuts; my Roza —3 four-layer cakes (one to be orange); Beatrice Lawler— grape tarts . . .

Maud interrupts to say she is not interested in cakes but in characters. Take for example Mr. Case. Would he not like to see a dream-bride walking slowly toward him in the crystal ball? Might not this expectation change his personality for the better?

Or take my Roza. Maud will tell her that this is the happiest period of her life and she sees something wonderful is coming her way, so—Beware of Change. How much would that be worth to me? I assure her it would be beyond price.

Take Charles, continues Maud. What would I like for him? I suggest that his home is threatened; that he is putting his trust in a weak reed; there is danger. Maud says that is a tough one but she will do her best.

At this moment last subject strolls in looking extremely pleased with himself as he announces that he has found out that Toona can make cocktails, and why didn't I tell him.

Toona follows with display of her talent on tray, and Charles, with a considerable amount of sipping and savoring, makes a couple of highly subtle criticisms which seem to give Toona a somber pleasure.

Walk out to car with Maud and we agree to confer again. Maud tells me she will call herself Madame Abdullah and her costume will be a complete disguise. Fortunately Hick will be away.

Do think dear Maud is so clever.

June 14

Letters arrive which prove agitating. Linda writes that after college she is visiting both roommates because she sacredly promised. A friend will motor her in his car from second roommate's home, which is only three hundred and twenty miles from us—so it shouldn't take more than a few hours—and will remain for a visit. He is absolutely terrific. I will understand him, but Daddy won't. Please ask Rachel to press her green dress etc.

Charles reads this at least three times with an inflamed face. Asks me to point out a single creep who has pursued Linda in past whose character he has not grasped far more swiftly than I. Try to calm him down but am secretly flattered that Linda is aware of my quality of comprehension.

Second letter, one of long series on visit of little Louise, is from Grandmother who writes that Louise will arrive by car on Saturday in care of chauffeur. Grandmother regrets she cannot deposit her herself, but she has a date. (Immediate vision presents itself of blue curls at a canasta tournament.)

Cissie thrown into panic over problem of how to get herself and Louise to Fair when time of arrival not specified. Assure her it will be arranged, but at the moment have no idea how.

Drive twenty-two miles to neighboring town in effort to procure delicacies demanded by Roza for cakes. Candied orange peel unheard of, and confectioners' sugar nonexistent. After strong appeal to de Boss, he consents to search for sugar in large town. To stimulate him, buy new-type Illinois cheese which I do not want and which is already over-ripe. De Boss says it is supposed to look like that.

Go into department store and purchase shorts for Cissie. Do not dare risk dress for Rachel without her presence. For no reason then find myself hanging over fake jewelry counter and am prevailed upon to try on pair of earrings like bird cages. Do not want them and receive cold look from sales lady as I slide away.

Go to gramophone department and relax while listening

to record called background cocktail music, with a tenor voice intermittently telling me to be sad, not glad, till He comes My way, Our way. Find am deeply moved by this, and buy it. Am disconcerted when salesman tells me it is a great favorite now with all the women.

Stop at Mary Jane's Beauty Shoppe and make appointment for hair following day. Antie says Well I am a stranger, and then adds she is coming Saturday to buy a cake. As she is first person who has offered to be a purchaser, am properly grateful and add manicure to appointment, for as Antie says Hands must be dainty when handling Sweets.

On arrival home take new-type Illinois cheese to Roza who eyes it with a What Next expression. Make mistake of asking her where Toona is. Roza dramatically closes door and then utters the words 'Scandinavian tramp.' Have no desire to have this clarified so merely give vague comment Oh surely not, and change to candied orange peel and confectioners' sugar.

Search out Toona and find her doing enormous cleaning job of my bedroom—windows wide open, rugs hanging out of them, mattress upside down in a spiral, floor wet from soapy water; whole appearance suggesting disinfection after smallpox case.

Say 'Good' as though it had been in my mind to have this done, and then to prove that am on top, hand her three dresses and ask that they be pressed before table set for supper.

Am quite proud of myself.

Prunes for dessert, and Charles asks Why, but Rachel saves the day by saying that she Loves Prunes. (How is it possible that in twelve years have never been aware of this fact?)

June 16

Charles receives telegram from editor of National Magazine asking him to come to city immediately for important conference.

Charles tells me he has no intention of interrupting work, even for a day. He knows how editors of national magazines operate when they are after articles. Eager revisers suggest changes, and wish to touch up and dramatize in order to reach 'our larger public.' This book, Charles cries, is not that kind of book.

Say nothing but go and telephone to de Boss about sugar. Ten minutes later Charles calls to ask where I have hidden his blue suit. Find it where it always hangs, and as Charles packs, he says he thinks my judgment is right and that it never hurts to talk to an editor. (Masculine mind in operation very devious as have no recollection of ever making this statement.)

Deposit him at station and show control by not asking him to do various vital commissions for me in city. Am struck at how anyone Leaving the country always looks so blithe.

Round up cake givers with final directives and call on Maud. Her house, which gets black mark from Julie, is exactly what I secretly covet—small, chintzed-up and resembling the better ads for linoleum, or contour sheets.

Find Maud encircled by scarves, shawls, veils, and beads. View tent which agree will look less like Boy Scout's home when covered by oriental rug, but am a little troubled that patrons will have to squat on ground as it is so low. Maud however shows me stool and says it is adequate for any weight.

Am impressed at how clearly Maud has made her plans when she produces small electric torch lamp, to be covered by piece of purple chiffon to give faint eerie light, though Crystal Ball appears a little small to hold the visions that it must disclose. We then arrange a simple set of signals. I will raise voice identifying cake purchasers who appear likely to enter (or crawl into) tent. When it is complete stranger and can furnish no clue to Maud, I will merely say that I hear Madame Abdullah is remarkable.

Maud gives me examples of her Egyptian accent, and who am I to say that it is not the purest of Nile inflections.

Round up sugar, have hair-do, and after supper read the Scarecrow of Oz to Cissie, which Rachel and I, though neither admitting it, find equally interesting.

June 18

Go to 'Last Day' school exercises and cannot agree with many mothers and four fathers (must remember to tell Charles) that it has been inspiring occasion. Wish I had the moral courage not to stand when God Bless America is sung, which position should be reserved only for National Anthem.

Mr. Parsons joins me afterwards and asks if I will step out to grounds and see if stand for cakes satisfactory. It resembles guillotine and I beg him to reduce size and lower height, which he has no desire to do. Request space near me be left for Fortune Teller, and Mr. Parsons pulls out paper and says it is not on list. (Would think Maud would have cleared this somewhere.) Tell Mr. Parsons we are very lucky in securing Madame A. who is donating services, and that she is most remarkable. Fear I will be trapped in tissue of lies so leap into further falsehoods by saying that Charles and I sat up all night studying estimate of alterations, and though it still seems rather high, want to talk to him immediately. Mr. Parsons forthwith becomes as honey in the horn and says he is going to buy one of my cakes as he knows from school meeting I must be an A-1 cook, and where do I want the Palmist to sit?

Rush home and call up Maud. Explain in low voice that if Mr. Parsons enters tent she is to use her ingenuity and prophesy dire results unless he cuts down on price of certain house, and then perceive vision of Our place in Ball. Maud, sounding a little distracted, says she will try but she is having an awful time at the moment with her costume, and do I think old black ski pants will look strange under yellow and gold mantle?

Children jubilant over end of school. Rachel refers to Miss Licks as that old Minotaur, and Cissie not to be outdone, happily screams she is glad she won't have to look at that Boa Constrictor Mrs. Whaley any more, No Sir. Would think they were both drunk were it not that memory faintly recalls similar elation on my part in these circumstances.

Charles telephones and I open my end of conversation by asking him how much money he thinks he will get. Charles answers that this has not crossed his mind (which is obviously absurd) and that he merely had a pleasant 'exploratory' talk with editor. Says he must hurry now to join editor, publisher, and Another woman for little dinner. As first woman not mentioned, am nonplused, or is publisher also a woman?

Having finished own supper with children a good hour

ago, do not like picture of Charles' evening at all. Am slightly cheered when he says he hopes to return tomorrow.

June 19

Early morning, which begins mild, turns rapidly warmer and find myself on school grounds placing four umbrellas over row of cakes on grass behind counter.

Tent of Maud is up with rug tied over it, which attracts considerable curiosity, and to standard query give standard reply that it is a big surprise. Other booths look gay and trimmed with far more imagination than mine, but best tablecloth with fillet inserts adds considerably to my decoration. Wish I had Rachel to help carry equipment on series of journeys to and from Chevrolet, but she is at house with Cissie, waiting to waylay car of Louise.

Stick a 'Sold' sign on one of Roza's cakes, and hope she will not arrive for some time as fear inevitable caustic comments on rival goodies will be delivered in loud tones.

As make next to last trip from car, which I finally succeed in backing up behind tent, sleek stationwagon with great amount of shiny leather, slips in beside me and extremely elegant man in tweeds alights. He gives me an almost hail-fellow greeting, and then pulls out from back of stationwagon rolls of wax paper, green and gold twine, striped boxes of varying sizes, and at the last a series of trays on which are patisserie, chocolates, éclairs, etc. that rival Rumpelmayer's.

I give squeals of excitement, and this benefactor, with an indulgent smile, tells me that as he packed the cakes it occurred to him that he should remain with me for the afternoon as he was convinced I would need assistance, and that Mrs. Pullman, Madam, was only too happy to acquiesce.

It is my old adversary, the butler.

Relationship I perceive has changed and that what once was scorn has turned to pity. Feel compelled to make volte-face in my own attitude though nevertheless keep attitude guarded.

Ask him his name and it appears to be Stratford-on-Avon (or something like that), but he suggests that I call him Herbert which he says is the way Mrs. Pullman addresses him.

In the midst of these disclosures, completely enveloped form appears from behind cars and glides in back of me. Follow figure into tent where I assist in the unwinding, and eventually unfurl Maud in total camouflage, and looking like an Iroquois in a harem veil. Whisper my congratulations but beg her not to frighten the children, as her appearance is truly awesome. We light lamp, place Crystal Ball on small table under its purple glow, and Maud spreads dirty pack of cards. Maud's fingernails are green.

Hang large sign outside tent—Madame Abdullah of Egypt, Fortune Teller—and await our customers.

Herbert-on-Avon studies placard and tells me that he was briefly in Cairo when Batman for Brigadier Hawley, in the El Alamein campaign of '43, Madam. Muses on bits of Egyptian dialect he still can recall. Interruption to this train of thought fortunately made by High School Band marching in with piercing clamor, plus appearance of Rachel and Cissie, panting, with Louise between them.

Grounds are now filling up, and with teachers, sales-ladies, and donors, almost suggests a milling crowd. Give three little girls spending money and peel off Louise's long flannel coat. Louise is plump and has blond curls which look as though would have to be wound every night. She seems unmoved by carnival beginning of her visit and wish she would smile a little in response to Cissie's excitement. Am ruffled when Herbert makes unsolicited comment that Louise is fair as an English rose. Do not answer.

Hissing sound comes from tent, and tearing in find Madame Abdullah on ground with palm leaf fan, in an atmosphere of intense heat. Says if I don't step on it and send in some customers she will pass out. Small group is standing outside tent and prevail on woman, who has purchased six brownies, to enter free as feel it is important for morale of Madame Abdullah.

Woman gives one yelp from inside tent, and comes out

four minutes later saying, Well I never did in my born days. Cannot imagine what she has been told.

Have in the meantime snared Mr. Case, who has been watching his brownies and is in high spirits over their success, and though he tells me he is a born skeptic, push him in to Madame A.

Lively sale now begins on Mrs. Pullman's offerings so am kept busy making change, and find Herbert invaluable in folding squares of waxed paper around circular cakes which I am not deft enough to accomplish.

Some eight minutes later Mr. Case totters out of tent with sweat pouring off his forehead but with nevertheless a look of flushed elation. He repeats Remarkable, Remarkable several times, and asks me how it is possible that his little abode could have been so precisely perceived in Crystal Ball as to even include an ancient burnt beam to left of fireplace, and the very chair he sits on when musing by fire.

But what is fantastic, continues Mr. Case, is that this dirty ignorant Egyptian woman, probably from some foul and evil-smelling gutter of Cairo, could accurately read these fantasies of mine and interpret their meaning.

Can see Maud has used hoary device of Bachelor's Reverie where wraithlike girls are part of curling smoke from pipe, and wonder at simplemindedness of Mr. Case.

The elder Miss Putnam now approaches with an even

more venerable friend, who expresses a keen desire to know her future. Lead her to the tent and she pokes her head in under the flap, then makes a sound like Pe-hew as though holding her nose, and quickly withdraws. Miss Putnam says she will return a little later with Pam-child.

What is the beginning of a cue now forms and boy at the end of line shouts that the dame inside the tepee has got cobras and is playing the flute. Restore order and am selective as to who shall follow whom. Cissie and Louise go in hand in hand, and come out with perspiring faces and apparently identical futures of marriage, with five children apiece, at which Cissie shows old-fashioned delight but Louise does not respond.

They run off together in search of grab bag and return in a few moments with Roza who wears old tulip-print dress of mine, and with a great deal more style. (Wish that I had kept it.) Make halting introduction between her and Herbert, and Roza as I feared, sweeps cookies and lady fingers aside, and plants her own cakes in dead center of table. Finally divert her toward tent for what to me may be the most significant Fortune of the afternoon. Fear Maud may not recognize her in finery of tulip dress, so say loudly: This way Roza and I am sure Roza you will hear something interesting Roza.

Am so tense over possible results, leave Herbert in charge of table and go to other booths where purchase pincushion, the inevitable sachet bags, birch-bark picture frame, and pink aprons for children. Find Cissie, with her arms about her teacher Mrs. Whaley, confiding her expectant maternity, to which the boa constrictor responds, Dear, that is just lovely and I couldn't be happier.

Buy two orangeades for Madame Abdullah as on last view her condition so sweltering, and the tent so reeking, dread she may collapse. Encounter Mrs. Pullman squired by Mr. Bromley, who as they sweep in give definite note of Royalty at last arrived.

Express my gratitude for Herbert and pastries, and Mrs. Pullman, with gracious wave of correctly gloved hand, says she believes in helping local efforts for indeed some of her best friends are the Locals and as I have been telling Estabrook They Really Are Delightful. Feel rustic dance should now take place, but Antie in a small feathered hat, and Mrs. Biltz sucking ice cream cone, do not seem likely material.

Return to table and one look at radiant face of Roza satisfies me that Maud must have delivered in a remarkable manner. Quickly hand orangeades to Herbert and tell him to take them in to Madame Abdullah; then ask Roza in as nonchalant a manner as I can muster if she received a good reading.

Roza grabs my hand and kisses it (a gesture reserved till now for Julie), and snatching up the orange-peel cake, hands it to me, crying: I give you this in gratitude, for I have been told a happiness awaits me, with you, Madame!

Builder Parsons who is standing nearby, in masterful fashion tells Roza he wants the cake and has already reserved it. Roza gives Mr. Parsons one penetrating look and then declares without any fight at all, which is quite unlike her, that he may have it. (Can Maud have altered her character?)

Herbert now comes out of the tent, and walking briskly up to the counter, announces with odious British clarity, In my opinion, Madam, that woman is an Impostor, and has never been to Egypt!

Try to silence him with an imperious gesture, but like a Back Bencher in Commons, he proceeds to heckle: She told me that I was a dishonest contractor who used bricks made of straw. My Word!

(Perceive that Maud has confused Herbert with Builder Parsons, and has wasted valuable prediction on a useless subject, which makes me furious.)

Say icily, That will do, Herbert; I think Mrs. Pullman is waiting for you, and then turn my back on him.

Feel the glorious moment has come to count my profits, so empty large jar—which is the bank—and find a surprising number of dollar bills between the quarters and dimes. Roza in some dream of her own stands gazing into space.

At this moment Rachel tears up to me and cries to come

quickly to the Fortune-Teller, Something has happened.
Realize that poor Maud is probably prostrated, and run
after Rachel.

Mr. L. the school principal is standing outside the tent
and in low voice informs me that certain irregularities
have unfortunately occurred, and he hopes it can all be
handled as quietly as possible. Am too startled to reply
but push past him. Maud, in full regalia including green
harem veil, is facing Dr. Root (the doctor that we do not
use), who in a voice of rising irritation says, All I ask Mam
is to see your Health Card.

This sounds like the Yellow Ticket and am so confounded can only exclaim, What do you mean?

I do not even know if she has been Vaccinated, says Dr.
Root.

Gallant Maud now rises to the occasion by turning to me
and croaking a series of words in some form of argot, which
I see is supposed to be her mother tongue, thus squarely
passing to me initiative for next move.

Dr. Root asks what she has said.

Decide under no circumstances will I give Maud away
to Dr. Root (who is Not my Doctor nor ever shall be), so
answer as coolly as I can, without looking at Maud, that
Abdullah is recalling time she was with me as old and
trusted washerwoman.

Dr. Root is not impressed and demands if she has a Work

Permit. He then ticks off on his fingers: Shooting Galleries, Gypsies, Mediums, Roller Coasters, Side Shows, Single Freaks or Monstrosities, must apply for work permit and be licensed before operating in this state.

I tell him in a shaking voice that Abdullah is Giving her Services so that has nothing to do with her.

Dr. Root snaps back that he is Health Officer here and I do not seem to realize that there are Children on the school grounds.

At this point I hear Herbert enunciating to someone with an even more precise diction: The moment she spoke, sir, I knew she was a Swindler! Step outside and there stands Charles in a new Panama hat, with brief case.

He hails me with the remark delivered in surprised voice, I had to walk from the station! This is so unrelated to emergency I cannot properly respond to it. Know that I am throwing up the sponge, but that something must be done as crisis in tent has reached climax. Kiss Charles warmly, at which he is a little astonished, and then say, You are next, dear; I promised the children and you cannot disappoint them.

Charles looks bewildered, but recognizing the age-old parental call to arms, hands me brief case and crawls into tent. Feeling quite depleted I walk away. Place myself in concealed position where have clear view of tent.

In about five minutes Dr. Root emerges with a very peculiar look on his face. Wait five minutes more and can stand it no longer, and go into tent. Charles is sitting on stool, and Maud is on the ground smoking a cigarette behind her veil.

Charles opens up with blast. So help him God he will give a hundred dollars to any good works I am inspired to help if I will keep my hands off them. What possible excuse have Maud and I to offer for terrorizing a respectable and timid lady?

Maud interrupts with explanation that on first woman that I sent in, she took a dry run to essay her own potency as clairvoyant, and had told woman, among other possibilities that third husband would be an African millionaire. The woman, says Maud, happened to be Dr. Root's wife.

Charles now demands that Maud throw off her disguise and disclose identity, in case she has 'wrought havoc,' as he calls it, among other innocent people. Maud and I refuse. Charles is adamant, says, This is a Serious matter.

Cissie's small face appears in opening of the tent, and she whispers that Roza wants to go home. She then more touchingly than any little Eva puts her arms around Charles and says: Oh Daddy, she has seen it in the Ball. I am going to have Five children!

Charles recognizes he has lost. Ignoring Maud, he marches out after Cissie, and I trail after him with brief case. We all get into the car, and little Louise climbs into the front seat.

Charles asks in anything but an undertone, Who the hell is This!

June 21

Worm out of Charles by show of avid interest that editor has made offer for piece if cuts can be achieved suitable to both him and Charles. Express wonder and respect, and attempt again to dig out How Much, but am cut short by Charles saying that therefore next three days must be particularly uninterrupted, and work unobstructed, so that piece can be swiftly gotten out of way and he can center again on real objective, The Book.

Try to match his achievement by telling him my table won a prize for second largest Take at Fair. Charles unmollified, unimpressed. Gathers armful of papers and as he marches out to study announces he may even eat by himself off tray in room to keep concentration at high pitch. Please, no diversions, no plans, no telephone, no children.

Cissie comes into bedroom. Says she wants Louise to go home. I state the obvious, that Louise had been with us for only one night of week's visit. Cissie replies that the only desire of Louise is to tag after Rachel, and Rachel keeps saying Butt out, and slams door.

Inquire if there is not some other form of diversion that would interest Louise, but the list embraces only what does not entertain her: not croquet, not visit farm, not play house, not hide from Roza, not paint, not eat graham crackers. All Louise wants is to tag, and Rachel, the last time she opened her door said, Butt out or I will kill you.

Cissie gives me trusting look and repeats will I please send Louise home. Ask Cissie why (would like to add the hell) did you want her so much, and Cissie says because she is my best friend.

Search out Louise and find her crouched by Rachel's door. Rachel opens at my command and Louise springs into room whereupon Rachel repeats in monotonous voice, Butt Out.

Remove Louise, who is quite amiable, and appeal to Rachel's better nature. End with corrupt bribe i.e. that if she will play with Cissie and Louise for today and take them off my neck—Mummy is very tired—will finally consent to permanent wave. Leave Rachel engrossed in contemplating her hair in mirror, and Louise again in room.

Tear through kitchen, tell Roza to get something, anything to eat, for I am going Out for Day. Toona calls from laundry tub in effort to block me off but I outwit her by diving through side door.

Drive to Mary Singer's for long-standing engagement to lunch and to my joy find her waiting with small picnic basket. Says she must get away from Her house as intensely serious assistant there correcting examination papers. Calls airily to shell spectacles bent over desk to cut all corners in order to pass everyone humanly possible.

Mary S. takes me to rocky ledge halfway up small mountain. Lovely landscape marred only by distant view of my house which looks shrunken and reproachful. Fortunately space too great to see figures but nevertheless decide to face the other way, with back to tree.

Over hot coffee from enormous thermos I find myself telling Mary S. that my life is a failure.

Mary S. looking a little startled says surely not, she always thinks of me as the most fortunate of women. I explain that I am, but due to own awful inadequacy constantly fall short of what her ilk call the Challenges.

In the first place I have none of the home-making skills illustrated in women's magazines, such as following a dress pattern, or papering a room. When I cook, I want to be left alone to cook like a cook, and eat by myself, and not be a smiling face over a bungalow apron.

And as for what is called Education, large sections have simply faded out. I can name the Graces, and make a stab at the Muses, and I can recite the Presidents, but only in sequence, and to place say Millard Fillmore, I have to approach him under my breath through Harrison, Tyler, Polk and Taylor.

[96]

Mary S. asks with some curiosity why I Want to place Millard Fillmore, and I explain it is just an example, like seven times eight—quick.

In the Humanities, I make the most awful Gaffes. The other day, in front of Charles, I mixed up the Brontës with Jane Austen. What I read, I do not Retain. My mind is as marble to receive and wax to hold.

Take languages. Once I spoke French a little, or think I did, and it is gone with the wind. So how do I meet this situation? I go to any length to cloak my ignorance. If the crisis arises which forces me to have a conversation with a Frenchman, I punctuate his observations with *Enfin ?, Incroyable, C'est un goût spécial,* and *Ça dépend des circonstances;* and very useful have these phrases proven, particularly if accompanied by an attentive smile.

As for common knowledge, I am pathetic. When it is indicated in a book that a character uses four-letter words (conveyed by dots, or stars), I honestly do not know what the words are, and I am ashamed to ask because it would be an admission of my simplicity.

And the reason for these failings, I cry out, is a very obvious one. My brain is never used, for only two demands are made of women like me—to raise Children, and to raise Money.

Having gotten this off my chest, I feel quite cheerful, and pour out some more coffee.

Mary Singer looks at me and then over the hills, as she pronounces in a severe voice, Any woman who has had your opportunities does not need to be a scatter-brained hen.

Inform her that the problem is not as simple as it sounds; I am not a scatter-brained hen, but rather a wool-gathering moon calf. I like to Pretend that I am brilliant; and I go into fantasies where I confound Society (in French) by my *esprit,* while receiving flowers and requests from the statesmen of the world for my good offices in assisting them in their careers.

Believe you me, Mary Singer, I announce, it is not Youth who dreams—the poets to the contrary. It is those of the dark Middle Ages who take off on flights of fancy to escape their own reality, which in the end leads them nowhere, and finally grounds them in a crash landing.

Mary Singer now becomes the Professional and rather brisk about it. Why don't I Do Something about my shortcomings. Why don't I discipline myself? Tell her that when I hear her, I am only thankful that my school days are over. And please not to tell me that Life is the greatest school of all because I too have attended commencements.

We then finish the coffee and go deeply into the subject of Mr. Pullman who we both agree is the bottom. Mary S. tells me he sent her three addresses, one, bound in leather, called Questions That Must Be Answered.

Drive over to Maud's on way home to ascertain condition of her health and find her with Hick and Charles, sitting under tree drinking juleps. Maud puts finger to lips which I assume means that Hick not yet apprised of Abdullah. Charles says he had been anxious about me and gives curious non-sequitur So that is why he is drinking with Hick and Maud.

Play conundrums after supper with children. Why is your nose in the middle of your face? Because it is the scenter. If you were to ride a donkey what fruit would you resemble? A pair.

Cissie offers these and then explains them to Louise who gives a delayed-action laugh ten minutes later.

Rachel contributes, What is the difference between a pretty girl and an apple? The apple you squeeze to get cider, and the pretty girl you get side-her to squeeze.

Charles says he simply must get back to his writing, and goes off to bed.

June 26

Toona says the country is awfully quiet.

June 28

Builder Parsons arrives in latest model Buick and carrying new sheaf of typewritten pages, and basket of sample plastics, color charts, etc. Feel justified in interrupting

Charles, who objects, but will not allow alternative that I go it alone on decisions.

Brief discussion between the three of us along familiar lines: that the best is the cheapest in the long run (from Mr. Parsons); let us do only basic minimum essentials, but well (from Charles); let us do Everything one coat, and on the cheap, because Who Knows what will happen to any of us in a year (from me).

Charles who is invariably unsympathetic to the Who Knows or What Does It Matter philosophy, blocks this while Mr. Parsons watches with foxy expression trying to assess on whom he will place his chips. Finally he jumps in with statement, delivered in soothing voice, that both are right; it is folly 'in these days' not to take advantage of marvelous economical synthetics—but on the other hand, with a rotting old house, bone work reinforcements must be of the best.

We finally agree (or rather I force them) to start with kitchen. Charles, Mr. Parsons and Roza listen as I explain new canned-gas units for cooking, built-in electric oven, new lighting system, walls to be yellow (three coats), windows thrown out into big bay with cute round table for us to eat breakfast on in sun, all ancient cabinets removed, and one low counter installed. Feel like inspired orator, gather momentum as I go on, and perceive Mr. P. almost kneeling as convert in front of me.

Roza gives a roar. The old coal stove is a wonderful stove, she understands it and this is the first time I have complained over what comes out of it. She Likes present cabinet because she knows where to find things; she does not want any family she works for sitting in her kitchen around cute table in sun—in fact she does not like sun anyhow but prefers present system of exposed electric bulbs hanging on cords from ceiling. Also, dark brown on walls is her favorite color.

Feel have lost battle and really hate Roza, when aid arrives from most unexpected quarter. Charles goes over to coal stove, kicks it, hits brick chimney, and asks Why could this not be jolly open fireplace for chilly days?

Mr. Parsons, now resembling sensitive Diplomat at international conference, quickly recognizes with which Block to throw in his hand. He walks over to Roza and in a sort of chuck-you-under-the-chin manner says, Now Miss Roza, that beautiful cake I bought will taste even finer when baked in new waist-high electric oven unit (sounding like best commercial on radio).

Roza again goes into curious trance observed by me at Fair, and after a moment replies quite gently to Mr. Parsons that she has never seen waist-high oven unit. Jump into my car, cries Builder Parsons, and we will look at one. (Names town some forty miles away.)

Fifteen minutes later, Roza in tulip-print dress drives

off in Buick, and rather sourly Toona cooks lunch and I do beds.

Roza does not return until nearly six and says she thinks it is better economy to order two ovens because 'you never can tell.' (Am sure this is direct quote from Mr. Parsons and do not know why but have uneasy feeling over alien influence.)

June 30

Take Cissie, Louise, and Rachel to 6 o'clock movie. Tell Rachel her hair honestly looks better without permanent but will live up to promise. Movie full of muscular hands around beautiful women's throats, and great hit with children. Have sodas and on return find Lawlers, Maud, and Hick, with Charles searching for poker chips.

Chips finally discovered in Cissie's room with little faces crayoned on the whites. Find old green camping blanket, which looks like baize, and place it on dining-room table. (Am quite proud of this rather sophisticated effect and hope the Lawlers are impressed.)

Hick wins and Beatrice is the big loser, and is not very sporting about it. All my bluffs fail except against Charles where by exhibition of false girlish excitement over my hand he drops with three of a kind, and I win large pot with two low pair. Am pleased about this.

Talk about best model pick-up trucks, School Fair, and McCarthy. Hick and Charles want to Do Something more about McCarthy. Maud says he will fade. Joe Lawler says you may not like his methods but someone has to clean house to clean out these Communists, and I with glassy eye fixed on Joe Lawler, cry the fault lies with the Administration which has shown No Courage.

Joe Lawler puts his horrid fat hand over mine and says I am an egg-head. (Joe is practically bald.)

Beatrice L. contributes statement that where there is smoke there must be fire, and adds that everyone would be behind Old Joe for the swell job he is doing if it weren't for the Leftist press.

(Feel have heard this conversation many times before, and will hear it many times again.)

As go to bed ask Charles how in these days one can live up to ancient Laws of Hospitality which dictate: As host one cannot insult guest in one's own house; as guest one is not supposed to insult host in his home; and a woman cannot ask a man to please step outside. Also if I am an egg-head, Beatrice Lawler is a pin-head, and wish I had called her that.

Charles very unsatisfactorily answers that she is a damn good-looking woman.

JULY

July 2

Sense atmosphere of household a little uneasy, so ask
Toona if she would like little son Gregory to come for
brief visit. Toona says Gregory he got big job now at $86
a week, plus tips, at country club. Goes to club hop Saturday nights. Boss wants him in Miami next winter.

Show teeth in smile and say How Lovely. Toona replies
she got sore back today. As with all conversations with
Toona, I exit rapidly.

Phone rings and there is familiar buzzing and clicks, and
after I have been identified masculine voice announces:
Sergeant Tremont speaking; Connect with Major Sylvester,

Headquarters, for call placed at 14:05; Party on wire. More crackles and I hear the Major's voice.

He extends on behalf of the General and Mrs. McQuinn invitation to luncheon for Charles, myself and two daughters, on July 21st, Transportation will be furnished.

Foolishly say we have a car, but Major repeats firmly Transportation will be furnished, and list of Guests and Program for day will be sent. Express deep gratitude the children included, and Major replies in adamantine voice Good-by Now, and clicks. See that with military no time may be wasted.

Charles pleased at prospect, but perceive it would have more significance for him if not a family jaunt. Asks me— as I appear to be going out—if I would mind driving to town that has good stationery store, the town that is 34 miles away, and there buy him one large Ms. envelope, for piece for editor. I suggest I buy three, and Charles answers that with coming alteration of kitchen we must observe the strictest economy in all directions.

Drop Rachel at Mary Jane's for permanent, and Rachel, in gracious mood, suggests that panting Louise remain to watch and they will walk home, yes carefully, yes Mummy on the left side of the road.

Cissie, on drive to stationer's, explains certain aspects of Louise to me. Louise loves Henry who is mama's husband and is jolly, but Auntie Sue who is papa's wife is only all right, and Auntie Sue's own son called Fredge or Cadge—Cissie is not sure which—is simply awful. Grandmother is papa's mother and she gives Louise presents all the time, and drinks.

Am quite horrified at this account and find myself on the 'isn't that sad' note immediately. But Cissie says Louise does not find it so at all. Louise does not remember very clearly when it was different, and pities Cissie because she has only one home. Because when Cissie explained we did have an apartment in the city, but it was rented, Louise said that did not count, and poor Cissie has only one home to go to.

Before supper Toona appears with first smile on frosty face and announces the guests have arrived, and then reads from paper 'Madam Pamela and Madam Louie-Louise.'

Rachel enters in evening dress of mine, hair in hundreds of tight ringlets, followed by Louise in dress of Linda's, her golden curls completely shorn, and resembling small Flemish boy.

Effect on Louise is as of one blind drunk with ecstasy, and causes her to be loquacious and facetious to the point of even essaying a conundrum which has no point, and causes her to go into convulsive giggles. It is Samson in reverse, and wonder if psychiatrists may have missed fine point in failing to suggest snipped locks for the insecure.

Louise darts off to kitchen to show Roza, and I ask

Rachel with justifiable indignation how I am to square this with four parents who have entrusted their child (Charles mutters Passed the Buck) to me? Rachel, proud of her master stroke, which she adds hastily I am to take out of her allowance, assures me that she has already instructed Louise that if she is with Mama she is to say Auntie Sue wanted her to have the New Look, and if she is visiting Papa she must say that Henry initiated it. Grandmother fortunately never notices anything because she is always going out.

July 4

Fireworks display at the Tracys', and Charles and Hick, in dark glasses, and wearing heavy gloves, struggle with giant pinwheel which will not turn. Suggestions hurled at them from audience, admonitions and advice fill the air, when small boy, escaping from his mother, rushes forward and with his little bare fist whirls pinwheel successfully.

On return home am met by Toona. Scene is brief, and closes with the curtain line: Very well Toona, then there is nothing more to be said.

July 6

Ms. of Charles mailed to editor and Charles rashly discloses probable financial reward which is in four figures.

Am awed as had no conception that what Charles thinks could be considered that valuable. As though it were finger of God, envelope brought in by Roza which holds latest estimate from Mr. Parsons. Final total on third page is lower than figure Charles has divulged.

Fierce argument ensues in which words such as retrench-ment, thrift, rainy days, and parsimony, are bandied about. Remind Charles that he cannot take emolument with him to he knows where, to which Charles responds that if that is really the case he has decided not to go there anyhow.

Compromise solution in offing when Charles takes Parsons' estimate and heavy red pencil and retires to study.

Cissie creeps into bedroom and whispers that Louise wishes to prolong visit, but I cry NO, she has already extended stay by a week, and Grandmother's car arrives tomorrow. Cissie looks relieved.

July 7

Grandmother's automobile appears, and I interrupt Charles, telling him that he must go down and wave Louise off.

Find Toona, in original travel costume, sitting on front seat of limousine beside chauffeur, with straw valise on her knees. Inform her taxi is arriving to take her to train, when Rachel screams at me that she has arranged this to save me the dollar. My face does not express gratitude but see am stymied, as Cissie embraces Toona, and Taffy jumps on the seat beside her.

Taffy removed, and Louise climbs into back seat, and my heart is suddenly twisted, she looks so very small. Can only hope Grandmother will be sober, and that her many homes will have the latch out.

July 10

Long distance call from Linda who in a blissful voice tells me she and Bowie—Bowie NORMAN Mummie—will arrive in late afternoon.

Repeat to Charles who, though skeptical of name Bowie, on the whole takes it calmly. Concludes, on what seems to me rather thin evidence, that Bowie sounds like Varsity hero, part of a cheer, and in spite of Linda's comment, he knows the type like the palm of his hand. All he will desire is exercise so Charles will arrange some men's doubles for tennis.

Point out that Bowie Norman is visiting Linda and that she may have other plans for his amusement, but Charles replies that Linda has no net and he has yet to meet the man who does not prefer men's doubles.

Rapture of all when at twilight Linda at wheel, in black slacks and pink shirt, drives in, with young man at her side.

Dogs bark with excitement and I, filled with an emotion I cannot explain, hug and kiss her and tell her that she is too thin.

Linda in voice that is surprisingly low for usual protest answers that it would not be like coming home if I had failed to say that.

Under Charles' supervision, Bowie Norman backs car behind tree and introductions are made. Bowie is small and ashen colored and speaks in so hushed a voice that first impression is of one coming out of ether, and having difficulty in articulating the words. Linda, with manner of protective dove, keeps large eyes fastened on Bowie's face, and tunes own speech on same remote wave length so that at times tones of both appear to fade out 'due to circumstances beyond our control.'

Conclude, as have often before with young men from the age of thirteen on, that Bowie is shy and must be made to feel At Home. This is not helped when Cissie asks if the cat has got his tongue, Bowie says Pardon? and Linda with vocal cords suddenly restored, cries, Cis, how dare you! Charles opportunely brings in tray of juleps, and welcoming atmosphere again re-established.

Charles now raises his glass to Linda and says the Old Man has missed her. A lot of surprises for her here including resurfaced tennis court. Big match tomorrow, and your friend Bowie is to make a fourth.

The Dove, with a whir of feathers as though distracting a serpent from a rabbit, exclaims that Bowie is writing Thesis for his Ph.D., therefore no time for anything but work 'while we are here.' Last phrase highly disturbing and am only thankful that no one picks it up.

We sit down to supper and immediately plunge into account of recent events, but give way to Rachel, the most vociferous, as she tells Linda of Aunt Julie's arrival, Toona's departure, Louise's home life, new kitchen, permanent wave and what does Linda Honestly think about it?

Sense that Rachel's news broadcast has not been particularly favorably received, for Linda's response is to gaze at Bowie with rather curious look, at which he ejaculates single word 'Maintenance' and gives her a compassionate smile.

Not unnaturally Charles asks what that means.

Maintenance, repeats Bowie . . . a generic term . . . a symbol . . . (voice fades).

Linda flies in, all feathers raised, crying, Bowie you are too modest—yes you are—it was sheer genius! You invented it—explain it to Dad.

Charles asks what the Hell they are talking about.

Bowie studies Charles for a few moments as though weighing his powers of comprehension, and then begins in faint voice:

Maintenance, sir, is a Protest aimed at what one might call the civilized world of today. The Protest concerns itself with the delusion of this world that they know how to converse. (Can see that in spite of himself attention of Charles is arrested.) Many of the allegedly intelligent believe they are having a conversation, when they are actually talking Maintenance. Maintenance, as defined in this so-called Protest, is the discussion of all material plans. The term includes talk of money, domestic problems, hospitality, alterations, plans for holidays, state of health, automobile, or wardrobe—the list in infinite. It may be necessary to discuss these practicalities, but it is false to believe it is conversation.

There is complete paralysis at the table, and Cissie looks as if she were about to cry.

The Sponsor of the Protest now gazes rather intently at Charles and continues: According to our theory (It's *yours*, Bowie, You invented it) it is permissible to discuss the mundane provided, provided, sir, one labels it audibly as Maintenance and is not deluded into believing that one is having a meeting of the minds.

Linda now clarifies it further. Let me give you some examples, Dad, so that you will really grasp it. . . . By by-passing the Parkways in the traffic hour I can make better time driving to the city . . . I believe in trading in a car every year, for in that way in effect you rent a brand new car for $294 . . . I have found an automatic coal-feeding furnace is better than gas—ten minutes of details supplied. (Charles winces.)

Bowie contributes *sotto voce* . . . I do not agree that the 17-inch television screen is as satisfactory as the larger model, but I am going to wait for color anyhow.

There is again a stunned silence and creator of the Protest gives us a threadlike smile.

And what, asks Charles, is Conversation?

It is I would say Sir the interchange of facts and ideas by the informed, given in disciplined style.

Linda gives a triumphant there I told you so glance at table, as Bowie adds: But of course there has been no conversation in the Western World for two hundred years.

Do not like expression on face of Charles, and try to give him grueling look of warning, as he responds in controlled and noncommittal voice: It is obvious Bowie that in your researches you have not read the memoirs of the Nineteenth Century.

Bowie however also appears to possess the art of hewing to the line, and is undeflected by that which does not appear pertinent. He inquires of Linda: Would you not agree that the last renaissance of The Art of Conversation of which there is testimony, occurred among the Encyclopaedists—Voltaire, Madame du Deffand, etc., he adds in an explanatory aside.

That's absolutely true, Bowie, is Linda's response.

Well if it is so lost, like how to make old mosaics, why bother? suggests Rachel in a helpful voice.

Charles rises heavily, and looking at Bowie says, I have some work to finish, if you and Glaucon will excuse me. This subtle shaft however is spoiled by his signaling to me in rather obvious fashion from door to join him. Cissie asks Linda a little timidly if she and Bowie would like to play parchesi.

Leave the Encyclopaedists with Rachel and Cissie, and take Old Joe and Taffy on stroll in order to avoid Charles and then find him in hammock.

Beg him to lower his voice.

In tones of stinging moderation Charles asks for how many days he is going to have to put up with this gas bag? Explain that gas bag is visiting Linda and I found his ideas enlivening. (Do not know why, but am instinctively on opposite side of Charles when he attacks.)

Charles, with an *et tu Brute* look, inquires how I could conceivably be enlivened by this Demosthenes exhorting the Western World in a whisper to step up its mental intercourse to meet the criteria of said authority.

Repeat that I was enlivened and found it salutary to be made aware of how much I talk Maintenance in twenty-four hours.

We swing for a moment in hammock when Charles

bursts out demanding how Linda—so level-headed, so astute—could have been taken in by such sophistry. Make error of telling him Rachel has already learned from Linda that Bowie is genius of University, and five publishers struggling for Book, called Philosophy of History, as yet unwritten.

Charles springs from hammock and says he is going to find Rachel. Beg him not to, as unfair to pump sister about sister.

Charles returns in three minutes leading Rachel.

Rachel, obviously flattered by position of confidante and advisor to her parents, sinks into hammock and informs us that (a) Linda in frightful state of nerves over what Bowie will think of family, especially—I am sorry—you, Dad; (b) Linda passionately in love; (c) Rachel not sure to what extent Bowie responds; (d) Linda learning typing to help Bowie with Thesis, and Rachel must not repeat, but she believes he will ultimately become President of U. of C. or Harvard. Rachel adds that she has been in Bowie's room. He has four shirts, no top to his pajamas, picture of Linda on skis, and half a bottle of Bourbon.

Charles listens in deepest concentration and then asks what They are doing now.

They, Rachel replies, are sitting in the big hall, and Cissie is sitting with them.

Charles wakes me twice during night, once by lighting

cigarette with three matches, the second time to ask if I am asleep, and if I am not, do I think I heard a car drive away?

Suggest he go downstairs and look, which he does not do. Asks me what I think is happening to Education in our country? Does not wait for my views but exclaims two four-letter words which I completely understand. Finally inquires of me if I do not think it is rather late to get into an argument, and he simply must get some rest. Immediately falls asleep, and I toss and turn until dawn.

July 11

Day so blue and cool am undismayed when Mrs. Biltz does not put in appearance at scheduled hour. Charles also affected by azure skies and dare-says he was a bit extreme last night; today he intends to relax with Bowie and try to enjoy him. Compliment him on being so reasonable.

Several Buicks and one Cadillac in turn-around and loud bangs coming from kitchen. Rush out and find scene of utmost confusion with Roza serving coffee to at least four extraordinarily handsome young men. Roza gleefully tells me we may have breakfast as soon as Boys have finished and see hint intended that I shall not spoil the fun.

Linda comes down, looking like a rosebud, and also in mood of reconciliation. Kisses Charles and tells us it is a beautiful day. First cloud appears when there is peculiarly loud crash from kitchen. Linda gives slight shudder and suggests it may disturb Bowie, but Rachel bouncing into dining room reassures her by telling us that Bowie will be down in five minutes, he is shaving and says he slept well.

Can see source of this bulletin does not please Linda but she does not pick it up.

Bowie descends a few minutes later and after gravely bidding us good morning holds toward me what appear to be three long pieces of matted yellow fur which he says he found in his bureau drawer.

There is a shriek from Cissie, Oh Goodie, you have found Louise's hair; while I am too horrified to speak.

Bowie, in a sprightly and out of character manner, takes blond curls and ties them about Rachel's head, at which Cissie screams, Oh Don't, She left them for us to remember her by, and makes a grab at the strands, thereby separating hairs some of them floating toward table.

Charles merely says my stomach is not very strong, while Cissie, near tears, retrieves locks and rushes from the room.

Apologize to Bowie at surprise in bureau, and Rachel comes to my rescue by saying that she 'Did' room but had forgotten to open drawers. Had assumed Louise had taken all hair with her in bag as a gift for Grandmother and the Others, and had not left instructions that there was a further bequest.

Charles now bangs on table and asks that the subject be dropped until he has finished breakfast, and can see that Linda and he are finally in harmony.

Perceive through window Builder Parsons drive up, with Mrs. Biltz and cat on front seat beside him. At welcome sight hurry out and waylay Mrs. Biltz thus preventing her from joining relaxed group in kitchen. Turn her thoughts to Rooms Upstairs. Place cat on screened porch with small bowl of water.

Return to kitchen and as I go through dining room hear Charles, in a completely unantagonistic voice, suggest that no religion flourishes in place where it was born, to which Bowie concurs, and Linda gives serious nod of agreement. (Can only admire Charles for achieving this heavenly accord in meeting of the minds.)

Mr. Parsons wishes decision on several minor points such as Why not new floor while we are about it, and Roza, unsecret ally, adds sinister suggestion of second sink. Return to dining room as feel need of consultation on these points and find climate has changed with suddenness and violence of a tropic storm.

Charles with warlike look on his face is exclaiming, You say *Toynbee* is limited?

We just think he Is, Dad, is Linda's soothing reply.

Toynbee, explains Bowie, accepts the partial historic information available to him as the totality of all history, and therefore most of his conclusions are based on false premises.

Want to get decision on floor from Charles but he waves me away furiously, so return to kitchen and have second cup of coffee with Mr. Parsons. Holes have already been knocked through wall in preparation for bay window, and sun, where never there was sun before, speckles the table at which we sit. Mr. Parsons introduces the four young men 'part of my crew' who have that scrubbed look of vitality of those who awake early and work with their hands. We talk of building materials—that new development has one-brick facing that crumbles before it's up, and the plaster cracks when you look at it; I wouldn't take one of those hencoops as a gift—electrical equipment and why those big shots can't get better television reception in this corner of the state is beyond me—spell of fine weather and this job ought not to take too long, that is if we don't run into any surprises, which you mostly do with these old houses.

Ask why in old houses surprises can never be pleasant ones, and am told interesting story that By Golly I won't believe it but there was such a house where a lot of old boarding, about to be carted away, turned out to be paneling which a dealer bought for four hundred dollars—remember Mr. Parsons?

Roza now tells a long and dramatic tale of digging for silver coins under cellar floor on ancient estate near Bratislava—We have candles, we dig, there is water, then there is iron box (pause—expectant hush) we open it, and inside is skeleton of small dog.

Mr. Parsons cries out in admiration, That certainly beats the Dutch, Miss Rosie, and Roza, flushed with success, pours out another round of coffee.

Can see that Salon which she and I have created is costing at least $50 an hour, but am loath to break it up it is so pleasant to be sitting in this attentive, responsive circle, with the newly achieved sunshine glittering about us.

Young man now enters and is introduced as Ed, my new sub-contractor. This has ominously expensive sound, but Ed wears steel-rimmed glasses, the symbol of early American honesty if not statesmanship. Ed wants a hand to get some coils out of truck, so regretfully party ends.

Get tray and make final foray into dining room to clear table. Linda is looking at Charles with expression of abysmal pity, as Charles cries, And I repeat for the Third time it is Men who change history, and not Peoples. I give you Napoleon, Churchill, Louis Fourteenth, Genghis Khan.

Bowie, with crucified smile, replies, If you want to take those rather obvious characters, sir, Kublai Khan had far greater influence than Genghis.

I am sure you must be right, Bowie, you are so much

younger than I am, is Charles' withering retort, which however does not wither at all. Bowie germinates a final thought:

There is one exception to the rule of races, as any serious student of the East soon discovers. Nothing of significance has happened in history comparable to the flowering of the Chou dynasty.

JOE, shrieks Cissy, why that's the name of OUR dog.

C-H-O-U, spells Bowie in racked voice.

Seize on this diversion and suggest we talk plans for the day. Bowie says (to my surprise) that he is going to devote morning to washing his car. Rachel immediately declares that she will help him because she Loves to wash cars, a remark I think she will regret.

Charles follows me back to kitchen, but suffering from battle fatigue has not enough vitality left to fight off new suggestions of Mr. Parsons, and keeps repeating Go ahead, in an exhausted voice. Find myself in strange role of advocate for economy, and announce firmly, with no buts about it, that new kitchen floor unnecessary, and second sink ridiculous.

Mr. Parsons shaking his head hopes I know what I am doing, Roza looks stricken, and Charles not unnaturally asks rather sharply why I ask for his advice if mind already made up.

(Difficult to explain in front of Mr. Parsons and young

men that what I want is his physical presence to back me on any decisions I make. Also am well aware that his exasperation at me is subconsciously aimed at Bowie. Wonder if psychologists understand this motivation as well as wives. Toy with idea of having Conversation with Bowie on this subject, with examples taken from over the centuries to illustrate how course of history might have been changed if King had not quarreled with Queen an hour before he declared war, or Prime Minister had not over-eaten, suffered indigestion, and as a result, at four a.m. broken diplomatic relations with five allies. Am fairly sure however that Bowie would deny the premise, and do not want to give the time to hear his arguments.)

Ed the sub-contractor comes to my rescue and says floor can be patched where coal stove stood, and second sink installed later if necessary. Perceive that Ed is a man of independence and give him grateful smile. Mr. Parsons however, showing that he belongs to the-best-defense-is-the-attack school, now requests Ed to go up on roof and he will see for himself 'what I am troubled about.'

(As roofs have never been mentioned before, and have never invited Mr. Parsons to wander around over them, consider this almost crooked on his part. What next? Will probably find him in the hall closet telling me my overcoat needs a new lining.)

Go upstairs again to crack whip over Mrs. Biltz and hear

her on screened porch telling her pussy Not to worry for if you are scared of those dirty dogs we won't come here any more.

Hear shrieks from turn-around and from window watch Bowie squirting hose at Rachel, as Rachel advances through spray and twists nozzle into Bowie's face. Cissie appears pulling a quivering Taffy and asks if he may be washed, when abruptly Charles' head appears in upper window and demands Less Noise as he is trying to work, then adds, after briefly studying scene, that there is no point in washing Taffy unless he is soaped first. From lower window comes tap-tap of Linda's typewriter.

July 13

Postman brings letter addressed to Charles. Engraven in left-hand corner is: Office of the Commanding General, Headquarters, John J. Pershing Army Base. Stamped across the top in red letters is the word OFFICIAL.

Consider this justification for interruption of any work and take it to Charles. We open it and find the program for our luncheon with General and Mrs. McQuinn.

Transportation will arrive for us at 08:45 hours (day, month and year given) at our house (road, village, and state included). We will proceed to MAIN-GATE Pershing Army Base, arriving at 09:41 hours, where we will be joined by the Hon. Everard J. Grindle (M.C.) and **Mr. George Pullman.** Colonel Lamar will welcome us, and under motorcycle escort we will proceed to MacArthur Airfield for the arrival from Washington, D.C. of:

Lt. Gen. Hatch (USA) and staff.

Senator Cosmo Wilkins and Mrs. Wilkins.

Maj. Gen. Peters (USAF)

Other Guests.

Plane scheduled at 10:11 hours.

Brief ceremony and review of Guard of Honor by Lieut-General Hatch.

At this point Charles and I are separated. Mrs. McQuinn and the ladies will proceed to Quarters One and attend short Coffee. Mrs. McQuinn, with the assistance of Lt. Swaine, will take the ladies to points of interest including visit to Day Nursery for children of Officer and Enlisted Personnel, Play Ground, Hospital, New PX, Thrift Shop, new Auditorium, etc. etc.

Charles' schedule is more warlike. He and the rest of the party, after ceremony at Air Field, proceed immediately by automobile for Inspection of Base, which includes visit to Barracks, N.C.O. Quarters, Hospital, Rifle Range, Side Arms Range, Artillery Range, Installations at Re-activated Army Air Base, including Helicopter and Liaison Planes.

At 12:04 hours, there will be a Briefing on Mission of the

Command at Headquarters Building, given by Colonel Sumpter, and illustrated with charts.

At 12:53 hours, General McQuinn will give a private Briefing in the office of General McQuinn for Senator Wilkins, Lt. Gen. Hatch (USA) and Maj. Gen. Peters (USAF).

At this same 12:53 hours, Major Sylvester will take the rest of the party to inspect photography installations and map-making facilities. (Am happy to see Mr. Pullman included in this lowlier trip.)

At 13:45 hours, Luncheon at Officers Club in honor of Senator and Mrs. Wilkins, and the Hon. Grindle (M.C.), given by General and Mrs. McQuinn.

At 15:40 hours, Reception in honor of Maj. Gen. Hatch (USA), by Officers of the Command.

At 17:20 hours, departure of Maj. Gen. Hatch and Staff, Senator and Mrs. Wilkins, Maj. Gen. Peters (USAF) and Guests, for Washington, D.C., from MacArthur Field. Brief ceremony.

Charles and I study this program for several moments in silence. Agree that it is unique opportunity. I find it incredible, and yet how typical, that George Pullman has horned in on this affair. Speculate as to how he got wind of it in the first place, and what brassy methods he used to secure invitation. Charles says it is a free country which is no answer at all.

Charles believes that General Hatch might be the Colonel Pug Hatch whom he knew in Malaya, and yet unlikely as nomenclature Pug stood for Nothing above the Ears, and improbable he could have risen so rapidly to the rank of Lieutenant General. Further believes that Senator Wilkins is on Senate Armed Services Committee, and purpose of his visit to Base accordingly not social, but to examine supply system of Army. Army in its turn can be counted on to demonstrate efficiency and economy with which it utilizes supplies made available to it. Feminine society result of presence of Senator's wife, Mrs. Cosmo Wilkins.

Inquire who the Hon. Everard Grindle is, and why if he is Master of Ceremonies, he has so little to do?

Charles looks at me pityingly and explains that M.C. stands for Member of Congress. The Hon. Grindle doubtless from this state and will later gain useful publicity by telling his constituents that he is personally responsible for lucrative Base. (Am constantly surprised at amount of information Charles possesses, but am forced to conclude that wide knowledge tends toward cynicism in one's judgments.)

Ask, without much conviction, if I might call up Mrs. McQuinn to see if we could include Linda, and Bowie as house guest, but received such an appalled look that I immediately withdraw suggestion and say I was only joking.

Turn to more important consideration of wardrobe.

Decide, after half an hour of holding dresses up to my chin in front of mirror, that lavender voile with small not very becoming white hat will have to do. Try on voile and find hem uneven, and dipping badly on right side. Cannot understand how hanging in closet has caused this. Start all over again. Decide on pink and black print with jacket which I do not like very much as fussy in appearance (Do not know why I purchased it originally) and large black straw hat.

March in to show Charles who says there is always wild wind on air field, generated by propellers, and will find it awkward when hat blows off.

Begin once more but know choice has narrowed to pale yellow cotton, becoming, but possessing grass stain at knee. Take dress to kitchen to consult with Roza and find there Ed the sub-contractor. Eyes behind shiny specs so intelligent, show him grass stains. He is reassuring, brings in can of liquid and says he can soak out stain in ten minutes. Explain crisis of proper costume for visit to Base and produce program.

Ed studies this with interest. Says he had no idea that old Buzzard McQuinn at Pershing Base. Was in his outfit during war. Saw him a year ago at reunion of Divisional Officers and General then feared he was slated for desk job at Pentagon.

Ask Ed if he would like me to tell General I have seen

him, at which Ed looks horrified. Sour voice from top of ladder outside suggests that before Ed shows his medals he should be so kind as to indicate where gutter is to drain, and Ed's face becomes redder.

Only slight ring on skirt where grass stain was, but believe with careful wash and press will get by.

Encounter Linda on stairs who demands if I am aware that Rachel has made Bowie drive her in his car to God knows where, and it is not Fair. Repeat Charles' statement that it is a free country, and then lure her into my room for judgment on hats. Linda cries, NO—Oh NO, as I display my wares, but finally concludes that if I will remove red ribbon from natural straw, and replace it with small wreath of green leaves, it won't look too awful. Am grateful for this crumb.

Electricity and water suddenly turned off, so luncheon of rather small sandwiches on porch. (Am convinced Roza has contrived four-course dinner for Mr. Parsons and his gang.) Charles looks at pitcher of milk and asks in incredulous voice, What is That? as though he were being offered some oriental poison. Bowie, after studying sandwiches, says he rarely eats lunch anyhow, and Rachel lets fall that she is not very hungry as she and Bowie had a marshmallow sundae at drugstore.

THE DINNER PARTY

July 16

Tennis afternoon carefully arranged by Charles, to open with men's doubles for one hour, and to be followed by mixed groups.

Charles, having been linesman once at a Davis Cup match, holds to a high standard of tennis protocol, and has managed to establish that all contenders on his court must appear in white, and Clean white.

The first arrivals are Hick, carrying three rackets, and his son Hick Junior. Hick Jr., who has added four inches to his height since Easter, wears dirty khaki shorts and small baseball cap. Can see that Charles would like to send him home, but is appeased when Hick Sr. tells him son is on tennis team of school, and fondly describes him as another Tilden.

Fourth man, local champion from club, has not yet appeared (am sure in consequence Charles will have him blackballed) so Rachel is ordered to get Bowie, and tell him to step on it. Rachel returns and says Bowie is taking a nap; Linda she adds has driven off in Bowie's car, and in reply to question where she was going had simply said, Oh Shut Up.

Am forced therefore to make fourth and am given Hick Jr. as partner. Immediately make forestalling apology to him as to what he is in for, and he replies that Oh this is a fun game, so what the dif?

Charles, who believes that the only purpose of any game is to win it, throws out three new balls and sharply announces: We will change on the odd, and will you please toss, Hick—recalling us sternly to our assignment.

We win toss but unfortunately the junior champion can only serve if he has all three balls in his large hand, and possesses such uncontrolled power that every serve goes wide of mark, and two over the backstop. Thus early in the match I begin to wear myself out chasing balls for my partner.

Situation rapidly deteriorates for our side as Hick Jr., like a young Samson unaware of his own strength, varies the high ones into the trees, with cannon balls into the net, and Charles begins to look very grave. Though he and Hick Sr. are winning, it is not the type of victory that is a triumph, and even I could wish that Hick Jr. would give up assumption that this is an afternoon for fun.

Charles now announces with great clarity that the score is *love* four, Your serve, and tosses the three precious balls over the net. The junior champ playfully puts up his racket to block them and again one bounces off, this time over the side lines onto Cissie's head, who greets it with flattering laughter, crying, Oh Do it Again.

Tell young Hick, trying to sound as much like his mother as possible, that he is to serve with Two balls and I want to Win.

Hick Jr. puts his cap on backwards, raises his racket as though to smite an ace, and then serves a short underhand to Charles, who rushes up from back line, and misses it. He then serves a twisting high bouncer to his father, who makes a great swoop, fans the air, and misses. We take the game.

Young Hick now reverses his cap again, and with the cruelty of which youth is supposed to be so cognizant makes his father and Charles run for small drop shots, hard, and we win two more games.

There is a consultation on the opposite side of the net and a new strategy appears of the middle-court game, everything overhead, and all to be aimed at me. Hick Jr. meets this by telling me to keep off the court, and then returns all balls accurately and hard down the middle, but angled to his father's slightly weak backhand. With frequent 'Sorry,' 'My ball,' Charles and Hick Sr.'s rackets clash continuously, and we win another game.

As the climax of the match approaches, Bowie appears, carrying a book with his finger marking the page, and sitting down on bench brings full force of his gaze to rest upon Charles, whom he inspects with the detached concentration of a scientist viewing a sport of nature which is deviating widely from its normal condition. Charles' game becomes even more disrupted by this, as he and Hick continue to parry the artillery of my partner, while I charge from side to side trying to eliminate myself behind the back line.

As the score reaches six all, other players of the mixed groups, including Maud, arrive, who join Bowie on the bench and in a violently partisan manner take sides. The amateur spirit, so beloved and hailed by all tennis veterans of Charles' generation, disappears completely as Maud shrieks to her son that she will pay him five dollars, spot cash, if he will only, only, beat his father.

This is the adrenalin that Hick Jr. needs. Standing twelve feet behind the net, he smashes four aces into the corners of the service line with the precision of a Bombardier, and the set is finally ours. Our opponents exhibit their sportsmanship by expressing only pleasure at the outcome, Hick Sr. even essaying to jump over the net to shake my hand.

Return to house to help with iced tea and, at sight of salmon-colored face in mirror, decide to take a shower. From bathroom window hear Rachel in her clear high voice saying, So I think I should go away because it is not fair to ruin my sister's life.

Peer out and see her standing by the zinnia bed with the two Miss Putnams (whom I did not invite), while above her on the roof sit Mr. Parsons and Ed the sub-contractor.

Love can be so Tragic! exclaims the elder Miss Putnam

with relish, and the younger Miss Putnam adds that You are so fine and so unselfish that I still think you will have your reward in the devotion of this good young man, Yes I Do.

Rachel however doubts this. Renunciation is what is ordained, and no one will ever know that the reason for her imminent departure is to remove herself as a rival of her sister.

(No one will ever know, that is, but the Misses Putnam, Mr. Parsons, Ed the sub-contractor, and me.)

Decide must somehow break up these confidences, so shout at the top of my lungs into the empty air: Yes Mrs. Biltz, little Rachel is bringing the iced tea to the court, and then have the pleasure of perceiving Rachel's horrified glance at my window as she swiftly guides the two Miss Putnams around the corner of the house. (Must talk to Charles.)

On return to court find Linda, in neat white visor and spotless tennis dress, playing net with furious speed and accuracy, with local champion as partner, against Charles and unknown woman. Linda receives rounds of applause as unknown woman shouts at Charles, Up! Up! and Charles goes down again to defeat.

Bowie is lying on the ground at the feet of Olivia Pullman and must at long last be having a conversation (or soliloquy) in the great tradition, for Olivia, no longer enervated, exclaims at least twice that that is absolutely fascinating and too too intriguing, and please do go on.

Second unknown lady, in perfect pleated silk, comes up to table and asks, Is that Plain ice tea? (Does she expect to have it laced with brandy?) She then adds how rare in America to come to an afternoon of such utter old-fashioned simplicity, to which I can think of no reasonably polite response as she eats four lettuce sandwiches which it took me an hour to make into rather fancy rolls.

Am then touched and also filled with remorse when the elder Miss Putnam shouts at me that this is a Glorious Fête, a real garden party. Prevail on Charles, who is sitting as far as possible from his unknown partner, with a bath towel around his neck, to bring both Miss Putnams back to the house and give them a cocktail. The younger Miss Putnam downs hers at a gulp, and exclaims that this is like the good old speakeasy days, which gives me curious insight into possible past.

Charles drives both the ladies home, and asks me on return if I do not find it rather pathetic the way poor old Hick plunges around the tennis court. Someone ought to tell him. Forbear giving a reply.

In the evening Bowie brings Charles two books, with slips of paper marking certain pages, and believes that if he reads them thoughtfully it will clear up some of his misapprehensions concerning racial predominance in the historic scheme.

Charles, by nature courteous, thanks him and Bowie graciously says, Not at all, but it is rather important, you know to have perspective when viewing the centuries, and not be deceived by the bubble reputation of the celebrity.

He then disappears with Linda, and they sit in car in drive for several hours.

Find him poisonous, feel deeply sorry for Charles, and decide that Crabbed youth and age cannot live together.

July 18

Linda says that Rachel ought to go to camp.

Olivia Pullman telephones, and asks if that brilliant Bowie Norman—and Linda—can come to lunch.

July 21

Start of trip to Army Base marred by Charles asking me if it is really necessary to include Rachel and Cissie, as doesn't it look pretty silly dragging children along to what promises to be a fairly serious occasion?

Point to program for the Day, which I now know by heart, and ask him if he doubts for one moment that plans for children not equally scheduled to the last split second.

Find Rachel and Cissie already sitting on front seat of

military car next to youthful corporal, from which position they are ejected by Charles who sits there himself. Beg children please to be careful not to wrinkle my yellow dress.

Presence of corporal has dampening effect on talk, and hear myself asking Charles in artificial voice if he does not find the day beautiful, though perhaps a trifle warm. Would like to include our driver in the conversation, but the uniform is that thin line of khaki which cannot be breached, and do not feel at liberty to secure my usual pound of personal revelations.

Cissie however has no such compunctions, and poking the corporal in the back, asks him how many people he has killed; at which the ears in front of me turn red and even Rachel is embarrassed, telling her sister in a hoarse whisper that he is much too Young.

Charles ignores back seat entirely, acting as though he were on a buggy ride with corporal, and engages him in so low voiced a colloquy we are excluded.

We pass through familiar scenery which is rolling and charming with green meadows and pretty farms. We then turn to the right on a wide four-stripper on which I have never been, and it is as though we were entering a new country. The soil is sandy and the growth is scrub pine, through which can be seen occasional wooden towers. On each side of road is barbwire.

Reach for handbag, take off hat, comb my hair and children's, replace hat, and apply lipstick. Spy vanity case in Rachel's pocket (Julie's gift) and whisper to her that if she Dares use it, will take it away from her forever.

We continue for several miles along road seeing nothing but pines, sand, barbwire, towers, and an occasional flock of crows. Pluck up my courage and ask Charles if he does not find this a little melancholy, to which he replies Not at all, and see by reflection of his face in mirror that on the contrary he finds it stirring if not beautiful, for he looks about him with satisfaction.

Abruptly the pines disappear, we are in clouds of choking dust, and going up a slight incline there is suddenly revealed a completely treeless area, several miles in circumference, and looking like the Sahara Desert. Across it are laid out with mathematical precision rows and rows of barracks and buildings, all of unpainted wood, while above the sun beats down from a sky of glaring whiteness, reflecting the arid soil below.

Marvelous, says Charles.

We drive up to Main Gate, two sentry boxes and forbidding signs warning us not to enter, but are waved in by the sentries who salute Charles, which he acknowledges by touching his hat.

(Who does Charles think they think he is?)

Behind gate are a company of soldiers, five cars in a row

with five drivers in uniform, and eight MP's in white helmets standing by eight motorcycles. To the left is a small knot of officers, with two civilians, one of whom is Mr. Pullman in large white linen suit. (How tactless to dress like an Admiral when visiting an Army base.)

Look at my wrist watch and it is exactly 09:41 hours.

Charles jumps out of car, moving away from his family as rapidly as possible, and shakes hands with a colonel. Look at schedule; of course Colonel Lamar. Colonel L. comes over to car, also consulting a schedule, and welcomes me and children but when I prepare to get out, tells me firmly please to remain where I am, as, consulting his wrist watch, we leave in 2 and $\frac{1}{4}$ minutes.

Assignment of seating now rapidly arranged and am surprised and happy to see Charles is placed in second car with an officer, while Mr. Pullman is two behind him. Colonel L. leads off with the Hon. Grindle.

There is a roar of the motorcycles, four in front and four behind, officer at head of company of soldiers all standing at attention, salutes (barely acknowledged by the Colonel and the Hon. Grindle) and the procession swings down the road.

Could only wish that Joe Lawler, Maud and about twelve other friends were standing on the wooden sidewalks, where I could acknowledge their presence by a slight lifting of my hand, but the only ones to observe us are a couple of soldiers in fatigues, and a woman hanging out laundry, who regard cavalcade with slightly cynical expressions.

Immediately ply our corporal with questions. Am conscious now that it is not his uniform but presence of Charles that has made me so circumspect, and find out his name is Stevens, comes from Wisconsin, married, wife expecting, formerly stationed in Germany (Germans cleaner than French), present assignment at Pershing Base no better no worse than any of them, all alike, might stay in Army for sake of retirement pay due in 22 years, on the other hand might go into garage business with cousin, but does not like cousin. Sure will be glad when today is over. That Colonel Lamar can be awful mean when Big Brass around.

Find these comments a little dispiriting and decide not to ask his opinion of General McQuinn.

Sirens on motorcycles now step up their lament, and with a final piercing wail procession roars onto airfield.

There, standing in formation, are company on company of soldiers, while directly in front of runway is Honor Guard at attention with the Colors. Sight so dramatic and so moving, tears spring to my eyes. Here is the Army which has fought all over the world. Here, with the ugly tar-papered buildings as background, and under a white and dusty sky, stand row upon row of the bravest of our country. Measured on any scale who adds more luster to the flag?

Remain speechless with pride, and a great sadness as to what may await these erect and sunburned figures. Where will they go in the next years and what will be their fate? And then added to my sadness is a feeling of envy. Of what? Of their youth? Of their manhood? Perhaps to feel that I was indispensable, instead of on any true count belonging to the first line of the expendables. I sit there facing the plain truth that I just do not count.

Our cars begin to disgorge their passengers and I see General McQuinn with other officers go forward and greet the Hon. Grindle, Charles, and Mr. Pullman. The three civilians look at a disadvantage next the uniforms, and even Mr. Pullman's white suit no longer suggests the bridge of a ship.

Get out of car with children feeling shy and out of place, and with gratitude see Dolly McQuinn approaching, whom I immediately find myself embracing. (Curious fact how acquaintanceship ripens by absence, and is then suddenly brought to full fruit by seeing new friend under strange surroundings, which immediately makes her an intimate.)

Dolly is followed by three ladies whom she introduces, names as usual escape me, but they are obviously wives of officers, and her lieutenants for the day. They wear very small hats while Dolly's is an enormous straw, thus clearly indicating that she is the wife of the C.O. (How foolish I was not to have worn my black cartwheel, and how right my instinct. I should never listen to Charles.)

The youngest lady lieutenant immediately grabs Rachel and Cissie by their unwilling hands and they are told to come with me dears, and we will wait with the other children. Cissie rolls her eyes at me desperately, but I can see from here on out we obey orders, and all decisions are being made at a higher level.

General McQuinn, who appears so formidable that I cannot believe I have ever met him, now studies the sky and looks at his wrist watch, and there is an atmosphere of subdued excitement. This is contagious, so study my own wrist watch and see with relief that all is still well as it is only 10:04 hours.

Major Sylvester detaches himself from the General and strolls (not walks) over to me and shakes my hand. Am indescribably grateful that he speaks to me and find this strong indication that he has an independent spirit. He and Mrs. McQuinn have quick consultation on 'finalized arrangements' and the word transportation crops up at least six times. Had no idea it figured so large in military planning.

Charles, who has been watching us out of the corner of his eye, and has seen the children successfully eliminated, now decides to act like a man instead of a mouse, so comes over also to greet Mrs. McQuinn, and is immediately followed by Mr. Pullman and the Hon. Grindle.

Mr. Pullman tells Major Sylvester that he is expecting a telephone call—from Washington—and Mrs. Pullman has remained at home for the express purpose of having it transferred to the Base. Will the Major see that he is immediately notified when it comes in? (Bet my bottom dollar Mrs. Pullman is going to Pretend to be Washington.) Major gives simple assertion, Will Do.

The Hon. Grindle shakes hands wherever he can find them and hopes I am happy at the Base. Have blissful thought he believes I am an officer's wife, and immediately stand very straight. General McQuinn now brings over his staff for more introductions. See with relief do not have to remember names, but simply look at insignia on shoulders. Find however have tendency to cling to Major Sylvester as my oldest and dearest friend, and that talking to this martial circle makes me quite fatuous, and I keep repeating in an inane way, It's all so thrilling. It really is!

Roar from the sky and a great plane is circling over the field. The appearance, though awaited, is so sudden and has such dramatic impact that my heart misses several beats, and I want to stretch up my arms and give it a cheer of welcome.

As it flies over us again at lower range, see it is a Constellation, and as it turns the black letters United States

Air Force stand out against the silver background, and clearly visible near the tail is the white star in its circle of blue with the red and white stripes extending on each side.

The soldiers hardly lift their eyes and I feel that I alone am finding the moment almost too agitating to bear, when Cissie suddenly breaks ranks and running forward, exultingly shouts WOW at the heavens, as she pinwheels her arms to hail the Big Bird.

(Cissie is my favorite child.)

The wings now cast their shadow counterpart upon the ground, and wheeling once more, the plane alights like an eagle at the end of the runway, and as it glides forward the reverse propellers go into action. There is a different sound, a duller roar of vibration as it moves up toward us, and then with precision stops opposite the exact point where General McQuinn is standing with his staff. The stairway is moved up, Army photographers poise their cameras, and breathlessly we watch the door.

Immediately General Hatch steps out and briskly descending salutes and then shakes hands with General McQuinn. Next appears Senator Wilkins, tall and perspiring in a Palm Beach suit and Panama hat, which he doffs as he descends the stair. Following him comes Mrs. Wilkins, plump as a pouter pigeon and assisted by the aide of General Hatch (a full Colonel) who carries what looks like a large knitting reticule and a pale pink jacket. (Observe

Major Sylvester eyeing Colonel-Aide with an ironic expression.)

Next out is a tall Air Force General in blue, and five officers of the Army; and at the end of the line appear two wrinkled civilians with brief cases, who blink at the scene likes moles emerging from a hole.

There is a short pause and a final civilian comes out of the door, in an impeccable white linen suit, who is anything but dim-eyed. He stands for a moment surveying the spectacle from the top step with calm satisfaction as though it had been designed for his pleasure. He lets his eyes rove over the group, and as they meet mine, he gives Me a shout and a wave. I am electrified, for recognize he is none other than Julie's Mr. Dighton—The Most Important Man Behind the Scenes. Without quite realizing what I am doing, I raise my right arm like Isolde greeting Tristan, and advance toward the plane.

Brought to my senses by Mrs. McQuinn's lady lieutenant grabbing me and saying, Honey, you stay just where you are. I move back fast.

Effort made by Colonel-Aide to propel Senator's wife, Mrs. Wilkins, away from the military and toward Mrs. McQuinn, which she blocks, and which he finally only accomplishes by jiu-jitsu on her elbow. Colonel-Aide then attempts to hand over pink jacket and knitting bag to Major Sylvester, saying in a commanding voice, Major, take care of these, to which Major Sylvester replies with almost a leer, She's your Baby, Colonel, and walks briskly away.

(Feel sure Major Sylvester will be broken in a matter of hours by this defiance.)

Band strikes up a march and General Hatch and General McQuinn review the Honor Guard, walking by the lines of erect figures at a quick clip. Staff officers stand at the left, Senator Wilkins moves in front of them, Congressman Grindle attempts to join him but is frozen out, and Mr. Pullman ingeniously places himself on parallel line with Senator, but closer to the cameras which immediately take innumerable shots of him. Look about to see position of Charles, and observe him standing modestly in background with Major Sylvester.

Children now wave at me violently from opposite side, seemingly finding it more exciting to discover me than watch the U.S. Army, but by ducking behind Mrs. Wilkins avoid catching their eye.

Inspection of Honor Guard is completed, and band plays Star-Spangled Banner. Everyone at attention, and moment is deeply moving. Peek at children and am touched at their erect figures facing the flag, with their small sunburned hands across their hearts. Army photographers also at attention, and recall the many other solemn occasions which have been marred by newspaper cameramen leaping over tombstones, with their hats on, to get just one more close-up of the bereaved.

Companies of soldiers march at eyes right as they pass the Generals, and by far the snappiest are the WACs whom I would like to applaud and whom Mr. Dighton boldly does.

Great activities now occur as cars are filled for tour of base. Major Sylvester is in charge, and no nonsense about it, ordering abject Captain to Put the Show on the Road for we are Behind Schedule; Captain blanches and shouts to Lieutenant to Get Cracking; Lieutenant answers Yes Sir, and gives incomprehensible order to three Sergeants in front cars, who wisely pay no attention.

Would like to wait and watch the loading but Dolly McQuinn directs Mrs. Wilkins and myself toward the green Ford. The recalcitrant Mrs. Wilkins however wishes to remain with the Senator, and as many men as she can snare, and puts a defiant hand on Mr. Dighton as her protector.

Sirens on the motorcycles are beginning their laments again, and Colonel-Aide rushes up and cries in a voice of panic: Mr. Dighton, sir, number 7 is now loading!

Mr. Dighton says flatteringly, Hell, I wanted to stay with the girls.

Mrs. Wilkins, immensely revived by this, figuratively slaps him on the wrist with a fan, and replies, Now, Now, the Senator is a very jealous man, and ultimately relinquishes her grip on his arm.

THE DINNER PARTY

The ladies are driven through bleak roads again, by bleak buildings, when abruptly we enter a green area with tree-lined streets, neat clipped lawns, and a series of double red brick houses with white porches. On each house is labeled the name of the occupants: Lt. Col. Barnes, Col. Hughes, etc. and it is quite clear that rank improves one's real estate.

At the end of the road there is an M.P. in a sentry box. He salutes and we pass through gates to the house of the C.O. which is larger, with bay windows, porches, and a riot of geraniums.

Inside are a group of young ladies, to my eye all beautiful, who are introduced as the wives of the officers on the General's staff. (Am increasingly depressed over the number of occasions I attend where the women are younger than I.)

Mrs. Wilkins now gives a scream, and says she has lost her Petit-Point. There is a scurry, and a pretty creature in pink cotton runs out and brings in the enormous knitting bag. Mrs. W. opens it, pulls out skeins of silk and a large square of canvas, which she tells us is the center piece of her fifth rug. Wherever she goes, whatever others are doing, she is always working at her Petit-Point. During the last campaign she filled in the background of a whole rug, much of it done on platforms while the Senator was speaking.

There are ohs and ahs of admiration, and Mrs. Wilkins unfurls from bag a huge roll of paper with scrolls over it, which she spreads on floor, and says is the over-all design, representing the emblems of all the States west of the Mississippi.

We exclaim again, and Mrs. McQuinn announces in her gentle voice that the Coffee is ready. But Mrs. Wilkins has her audience and will not be budged. She pulls out more skeins of silk, lays them on the paper on the floor so that we will understand the color scheme. We all say oh and ah again.

Mrs. Wilkins now says that she wants to let us in on a little secret. The Senator has told her that there is nothing prettier than a lady's hands when working at needlepoint. The Senator likes to look up from his papers and documents and see her needle flashing in and out. It is Feminine.

Furthermore, continues Mrs. W., Petit-Point has another advantage. It is a subject of conversation. Most people are shy when meeting her, and to put them at their ease she shows them her Petit-Point, and talks about it. She can often use up a couple of hours on the subject, and the shy ones do not have to speak at all, and before they know it, it is time to go home.

Pink cotton girl, who it is hard to believe has finished school, exclaims, Ah make mah little dog do tricks at mah parties. He ken smoke a corn-cob pipe. Mrs. W does not look overly pleased at this alternate sample of entertainment, and silently gathers up her skeins.

The Coffee is spread on the dining-room table with many little cakes, but as we are about to fall to, Lieutenant appears, and announces the fatal words delivered in a breathless voice, We are Behind Schedule.

Dolly with spirit replies, It Does Not Matter, but the pressure is on, and we are firmly mustered for the tour. The Lieutenant gives us innumerable statistics, delivered in a high-strung manner, and addresses Mrs. Wilkins as Yes Sir, I mean Mam.

Contretemps of serious dimensions occurs when the ladies' motorcade drives up to hospital and runs head on into the Military-Washington company. Our Lieutenant turns gray, Major Sylvester gives us a look of horror, and Colonel Aide shows obvious satisfaction at this example of poor staff work. Matters not helped when Mrs. Wilkins leaves the Harem and charges forward, knocking officers out of her way, to reach the Senator. Senator exclaims, Why Miss Linda Lou, Child, and does not appear at all put out. Glance at Charles to see if he is observing this courtly behavior, but he has turned his back and is studying Plaque on the wall to avoid any demonstration of recognition on my part.

Mrs. Wilkins is retrieved again and we continue our pilgrimage, in opposite direction, and inspect Thrift Shop, Commissary, and Day Nursery where two blue-aproned volunteers are in charge assisted by a Corporal, who in a thundering voice orders three tiny boys into the Clink which I discover is the toilet.

Deafening roar of gunfire brightens the Lieutenant who says, That is the Side Arms Range, and it is now safe to return to hospital. Mrs. Wilkins here puts her foot down and announces she does not wish to inspect any more but would like to sit quietly under a tree with her Petit-Point. Do not quite know how it is effected, but she and I are deposited in two deep straw chairs on terrace of Officers Club, while Dolly sails off light-heartedly with her lady aides, assuring us, like MacArthur, she will Return. (Cannot help but feel that something has been hung up on me.)

Petit-Point is once more unrolled and we go into it again exhaustively.

Mrs. Wilkins asks me if it does not make me nervous to have idle hands. Ask her in turn if she means that I will get into mischief, and she retorts, Heavens No, You are not the Type. Am huffed by this as am pretty sure I am as capable of Mischief as she is.

We then take up the subject of Mrs. Wilkins herself, and I ask her if it is difficult to be a Senator's wife. She replies that it is harder to become one than to be one. Chew this over and cannot decide if it is profound or not. She goes on to say that the Senator cares about two things only, his beloved State and Home Life, and that God has blessed her with the gift of home-making. Inquire where she lives in Washington, and she names large hotel on Connecticut Avenue.

Mrs. Wilkins now takes off her glasses, breathes on them, looks restlessly about, and wonders what is keeping the men. As a series of detonations of bombardment proportions are thundering about us, think she might guess.

Cannonade suddenly ceases. Dolly McQuinn appears in a new costume, and I am permitted to peer through hole in hedge where a number of children are playing a form of volley ball. Cissie is sitting alone on the side line, but decide not to signal her as fear I would receive immediate appeal to take her home.

I inspect club by myself which resembles deep-sea grotto, no daylight being allowed to penetrate and illuminated entirely by dim green and blue balls. Discover in furthest room chromium bar floodlighted in pink, at which are sitting Mr. Dighton, Major Sylvester and Charles.

It seemed simpler to be briefed here, Mr. Dighton explains, what will you have? I do have, and we are gradually joined by the civilian moles and Congressman Grindle. Mr. Pullman finally totters in, and sinking to a chair announces that he is completely deaf in one ear and has a splitting headache. Major Sylvester suggests a visit to the Map Making Facilities, but receives negative replies.

It is now well after 13 hours and I am becoming quite faint in spite of eating a number of peanuts, when there is the welcoming sound of sirens, and the Generals march in, looking fresh as daisies, and flanking Senator Wilkins to whom they are both talking briskly. Senator Wilkins has reached the stage of exhaustion where he can only nod his head, very slowly, in acquiescence to whatever is said, and am reasonably sure that this is the moment when Generals Hatch and McQuinn are securing that vote for even larger Army appropriations.

Luncheon takes place at a wide U-shaped table and is seated according to the strictest protocol. Am therefore astonished when I find myself next to the Air Force General, whose comments on today's activities I find acutely penetrating.

General McQuinn makes short welcoming speech to the Senator and His Lovely Lady (applause and we all stand up), and Mrs. Wilkins is presented with corsage, which she pins on with an experienced hand. Photographers snap her and I cannot help but admire the way she lifts three fingers in a small inclusive wave.

Brief interlude during which we eat, while 5-piece orchestra plays a waltz. Microphone is now placed in front of the Senator, which rejuvenates him like the Fountain of

Youth, mole from Washington slips up behind and hands him what looks like at least thirty typewritten pages, and khaki figure with earphones crawls out from under table and requests Absolute Silence as we are now On the Air. Senator rises, receives signal from Earphones, and is off.

. . . In this day and age . . . paramount importance . . . economy is the watchword . . . proper military posture . . . closely geared . . . the Fiscal year . . . waste and corruption . . . the Family of missiles . . . the marriage of atomic power to peaceful uses . . . the specialized nature of . . . the enemy without and within . . . the eyes and ears . . .

At this moment a Captain enters, and tiptoeing up to Mr. Pullman, delivers a whispered message. Mr. Pullman looking a little disconcerted, nevertheless rises but cannot immediately find his glasses which are clearly visible behind the coffee cup to all sitting opposite to him. As in all diversions during a speech, every eye leaves the Senator and fastens on Mr. Pullman and his search for his specs, with absorbed attention. Glasses finally discovered, there is an almost audible sigh of relief, and Mr. Pullman creaks out.

. . . The reservoir of power . . . the Arsenal of Democracy . . . the Prophets of Doom and Gloom . . . I am reminded of a little incident . . . the East and West . . .

World leadership . . . facing the crossroads . . . and now with God's help . . .

We all applaud, but are instantly silenced by Earphones as three privates are led in, looking absolutely appalled, as well as they might, at the array of Brass which confronts them, and are stood in a row beside the Senator.

Senator Wilkins now assumes a jocular-fatherly manner. You boys from my State? Yes sir. Give me your names and home addresses so I can write your folks the wonderful job you are doing for your country. Whispered replies which one of the moles takes down. Remember I am your Senator and I have the interests of each and every one of you at heart. Yes Sir. Any complaints? The Army treats you right? Yes Sir. How is the chow? Yes Sir. Son, I see from the emblem on your collar you are in the artillery. Yes Sir. I presume you saw your Senator fire that massive shell this morning. Silence. Were you not out there on the range with your comrades in arms to watch your Senator fire that shell! Pause:—We were ordered to take showers.

This reply ends broadcast and luncheon.

In the outer rooms a large group is already assembling for the Reception. In a matter of minutes it is organized and Charles and I find ourselves in a procession slowly approaching Generals McQuinn and Hatch. A subtle change however has taken place in their demeanor and there is an extra cordiality. General Hatch hails Charles as

Charlie-boy, and begs me to call him Pug, while General McQuinn reverts to the manner of our first meeting. He squeezes my hand, while he looks into my eyes, and then, as though he were Napoleon and I was the Countess Walewska, ejaculates the single word, When? Can only explain this enthusiasm of manner by the fact that the end is near, and victory in sight.

Charles' strength however is ebbing fast. Unwilling to relinquish the assumed role of an officer of high rank, he nevertheless has not the endurance to keep up the fight, and is now ready for the strategic retreat. He puts his hands on my shoulders, and mutters, Let's beat it.

Propelling me in front, he marches over to Major Sylvester and announces in a most snappy manner, Major, we are leaving immediately. Please furnish us Transportation.

Yes Sir, replies the Major.

Remind Charles we have children, which is a shock.

And have transportation furnished for my daughters when they have concluded their schedule.

Yes Sir, repeats the Major.

Last view, as we pass through side entrance, is of Mr. Pullman talking to the Senator, with contented furrow on his brow, while Mrs. Wilkins sits on a loveseat with Petit-Point and Colonel-Aide, who is looking at his wrist watch.

Major Sylvester places us in a car and I try to counteract the unfortunate manner of Charles by murmuring 'Memorable Day' over and over again. As we drive off Charles touches his hat again to six marching WACs, who respond with startled salutes. Turn on him to bring all my indignation to bear but receive a final directive: I do not wish any comments, favorable or otherwise, on me or the Army, until 18 hours;—and leaning back he closes his eyes.

Several hours later children are returned, in charge of Lieutenant. Rachel has arrived at one clear-cut conclusion. She wishes to live forever on an Army Post. Cissie is completely depressed. She was homesick the whole time. The girls all whispered and were silly, and Rachel was the silliest of all. They talked about one thing over and over again and then kept saying, Hush. Ask her what it was they talked about, and Cissie replies that she cannot tell me. She finally prints on a pad with a green crayon:

$$S. E. K. S.$$

July 25

Reaction after visit with the Army for several days is one of deep discontent with my dull life and prosaic family. Would like to be a Mrs. General surrounded by those of lower rank, to whom I could be gracious. Wonder how I would look photographed if I received a bouquet of roses. Am aware that this type of fantasy is weakening to the character so decide to come to earth, and face up to the problem that has top priority—i.e. Linda and Bowie.

Plan to have a little talk with Linda. Realize that I will tread on delicate ground and must approach the question of her feelings cautiously, but do not think it unreasonable to find out if Bowie is going to spend the entire summer with us, at the same time giving her a slight hint that Charles finds him horrible.

Rehearse rather carefully to myself what I plan to say and conclude that I will put most of the onus on Charles, while telling Linda how much I like Bowie, his intelligent mind, etc. Hope by this to win her confidence so that I can then point out that she is very young, and her life is still before her. Will conclude that all I want is her happiness.

Am not entirely satisfied as I go over my points, but after all Linda is my daughter and am sure she feels close to me.

Do not know why it is so extraordinarily difficult to arrange a private conversation with a member of a family, particularly if you do not want member to know that it is to be private. House undeniably has a number of rooms, but to decoy Linda into one and then close the door would arouse suspicions, and to sit in parlor, library or hall would be similar to thru-way at airport. No spot possible outdoors with Rachel and Cissie about, and Charles invades the second floor.

Finally I hit on a rather clever ruse. Ask Linda if she would give my hair a slight clip, as I wish to change my part to other side and cannot get an appointment at Mary Jane's Beauty Shoppe. Linda consents, though not over-enthusiastically, and we repair to back bathroom (closing door), where I sit facing mirror which also reflects her face.

Preliminary discussion of position of new part in hair which we do not entirely agree upon, but finally draw a compromise line, and Linda, twirling her scissors on one finger, tells me to bend my head forward. This position is a little difficult for conversation but decide its very imper-sonality lends itself to the casual.

After a couple of professional clicks with the scissors, Linda announces that she will give me a more pointed neckline, and that as my hair is not very thick, the whole operation can be finished within ten minutes. Debate how in this limited time I can reach the heart of the matter when fate plays into my hands. Linda continues that she rather likes to trim, especially men, and has done Bowie twice.

Am slightly repelled by this picture but nevertheless name has been introduced naturally, so remark that it was a kind deed as it must have saved Bowie money.

Linda gives a surprised laugh, and ejaculates, Money! Bowie is loaded with it. I cut his hair for training.

Ask Linda why he seems so poor, and she replies, Because he is an intellectual.

Time is running out so move in a little faster. Tell her I am so very fond of Bowie. Linda responds, Yes, he certainly can charm the birds off the trees. I go on and say, Of course you have so much to offer, dear. Linda asks, How do you mean? I then lose my head, jump the gun, and cry, All I want is your happiness, and my eyes fill with tears.

Linda throws down her scissors and exclaims, Mummie! Are you trying to have *A Little Talk*?

Instead of letting well enough alone, blow my nose, and say, If you really care for him . . .

Linda, her face bright scarlet, repeats, Care for Him! What a rent-book library expression. Bowie is absolutely right that all women over forty live only vicariously through fiction.

Am completely undone by the injustice of this statement as read at least one serious book to every four novels, and am now in the middle of Cecil's Melbourne. Ask her how she can possibly judge if I live vicariously or not.

Linda answers that I cried when I reread Gone With The Wind. She then adds that since we are on the subject (the nature of which I now have no idea), and are really laying it on the line, will I please stop Rachel from coming into her bedroom uninvited, and pawing through her mail. All she asks out of life is Privacy.

The irrelevancy of this request floors me, but tell her that when she is over forty and has a home of her own, she will find privacy impossible to achieve. Linda retorts, Not if one is properly organized, and combs hair over my face.

I say that children are the enemy of privacy, and she answers that she is not sure that she Believes in children.

Sense that this may be another Bowie aphorism and become quite agitated, not only over the potency of this alien influence but by the scissors which are snapping mercilessly behind one ear. Try to clarify my remarks which I feel have not been understood at all, and, conjuring up a phantom Charles for support, say that Daddy thinks marriage is a very serious business.

Marriage, shrieks Linda, Who is talking Marriage!

Am by now so shaken that I grab a Kleenex and repeat in a quavering voice, What I am trying to say is that all I want is your Happiness.

Linda gives what can only be described as a yelp, and cries, What I am saying is that I am Glad Bowie is leaving tomorrow, because I wouldn't put it beyond you not to ask him his *Intentions,* and rushes out of the bathroom, slamming the door.

One fact alone emerges from this stormy scene and I cling to it. Bowie is leaving. Tear across the upper hall to study and interrupt Charles to give him this news. Charles says, Oh yes, I forgot to tell you. You know I have become rather fond of the little guy.

He then gives me a stare, suggests that I do something about my hair.

July 26

Bowie leaves in the morning and am so filled with a sense of guilt toward him that I am extravagant in my expressions of grief at his departure, and beg him to please come again soon.

Bowie says he is afraid he will have to disappoint me.

Linda kisses him with no attempt at concealment, on his cheek, and says Darling Bowie, while he vaguely slaps her back. Conclude that relationship between mother and daughter is not close at all from daughter's point of view, and that I have not the faintest idea what Linda is really feeling.

As the car drives off Rachel emotionally blows her nose, while Cissie with great sincerity yells *Hooray*.

Go to kitchen, and Roza puts final drop of poison in my cup by saying, That was a wonderful young man, and a Millionaire too.

AUGUST

August 3

Rachel goes for a visit down the line with friend called Sally Barker, and begs to be allowed to travel by train, as she is more likely to have adventures on a train, and it is so terribly exciting to see who climbs on. I finally agree on promise that she will not talk to adventurers. Rachel says she would not think of doing that, all she ever does is smile.

As train is crowded local, think she will be safe, and I promise that will not put her in charge of conductor which I concede is babyish, but think I will tell him privately to shove her off at right station.

Rachel receives much advice on her deportment, beginning with my admonition to Stand Up when an older person comes into the room, from Charles to lay off the Tall Stories, from Linda that after she has used a comb to take her hair Out of It.

Tell Linda that that type of suggestion should be given in private, whereupon Linda groans that she shares a bathroom with Rachel.

Rachel asks what she should give the maid if there is one, and Linda competently handles this by taking new pair of nylons from my bureau drawer, and tying them up in a neat package.

Cissie begs Rachel to write her every day, and I ask her to telephone me when she has arrived, and to Reverse the Charges.

August 6

Desk piled so high with Unfinished Business, make up my mind to clear it up once and for all, and stop shoving papers under other papers. Get box of large-size clips from stationery shelf, elastics, small pads, and five pencils.

Decide, in order to move ahead efficiently, to sort out whole conglomeration into separate piles; so write on slips of paper: Bills, Financial (Bank statements etc.), Letters To Be Answered, Appeals, Advertisements. Band everything together with elastics under these headings, and am

pleased that the desk begins to look more orderly. As Bills and Financial will probably take the longest, plan to begin with the Ads and rapidly riff through them before throwing them into the scrap basket.

Find to my surprise that some of these notices are quite interesting, and conclude I am being too hasty and should analyze their suggestions more carefully; so make another heading on slip of paper: Possible Purchases To Be Considered. Have never possessed a fur evening jacket and the illustrations are extremely attractive, one-third less if purchased now, and apparently guaranteeing two shadowy men in white ties who appear behind the jackets in each picture, looking admiring and devoted. Must admit however that summer prices are still three times as much as I have ever spent for any wrap. Nevertheless will keep pictures if for no other reason than that they will Train the Eye for the new line.

Add to Possible Purchases To Be Considered, a half-dozen tempting sketches of nylon slips and nightgowns, some sample Christmas cards (again a surprising suggestion for August but might it not be an excellent idea to be so forehanded?), and an entire booklet on labor-saving devices for In-and-Out Doors, which will certainly need further study.

Pile of advertisements increasing so rapidly of P. Purchases To Be C., open card table and move it up next to desk. Throw out several circulars of new laundries, but open with anticipatory pleasure very large envelope from renowned international House. Enclosed are two letters on lustrous stationery which bears a coat of arms. The first, which is written in longhand in purple ink and signed Celeste, informs me that the Andrea Doria has just arrived, and implores me to drop by and select from the new Roman slacks in Gourmet colors. (Shades not specified but should imagine Burgundy or Artichoke.) Slacks, says Celeste, look like me.

The second letter is typed, opens abruptly with single word Madam, and brings to my notice that I am in arrears, statement enclosed to date of amounts owing (can see by quick glance that it must be inaccurate), all bills payable by 11th of each month, and concludes with sharply worded suggestion situation be cleared up immediately; signed J. Brown, Dept. of Accounts.

These dual epistles infuriate me for which role does famous international House wish me to assume in my relations with it? A timid client who will think twice before purchasing a lipstick, or a leader of fashion who wears Gourmet slacks?

Take slip of paper and write: Send curt reply to J. Brown; order 1 pr. slacks, Celeste, and then see what happens. Clip this to two letters and place them in packet 'To be Answered,' but at the bottom.

Next look over Appeals, and can see that they are closely related to Bills, if not Financial. Am rightly mortified that request to give a child two weeks at a summer camp, and probably mailed to me in April, is only now being scrutinized for the first time. Immediately imagine child is Cissie, quickly draw check and slip it into envelope, but band the rest together again for further study.

The letters To Be Answered are eight in number (nine now with contemplated retort to J. Brown), and after looking through them feel nothing is less true than old saw that if you do not answer your correspondents, they answer themselves. The converse would seem to be the case, that the longer one delays the more irksome it becomes. Fortunately three are from Julie, so can box these in one reply. Reread her last, from Kansas, where she says she is visiting French Countess (which sounds most unlikely), and that waving wheat fields reminded her of the Bible. (Think she should be a little more specific.) Proposes that she pop in on us once more before 'trekking to the frozen North.'

Think it simpler to telegraph her to come than waste energy on long epistle of family doings.

Charles' dear Aunt Rachel asks for ideas for his birthday present. Impossible to suggest pick-up truck owing to extreme sentimentality of Aunt Rachel. Check in three figures not feasible for same reason, yet if some direction is not given, leather-bound set of Works of Rudyard Kipling probably inevitable. Put letter aside and will talk to Charles.

Two of my pencils quite blunted owing to little sketch of sailboat I have drawn on blotter while pondering over Aunt Rachel, so take time to sharpen all pencils, and get a glass of water.

Look over Financial but simply have not the time to balance check book with Statement, and will therefore accept Bank's figures as more or less accurate, for if one cannot trust one's own Bank, who is there left to trust?

Can tell from the names on the envelopes of Bills that some are repeats, or in the vernacular, 'rendered,' which fortunately will reduce the pile. As I pull out one, somewhat in the manner of trying to guess which is the jack of hearts in a card trick, there is the welcoming sound of the luncheon gong, so put whole sheaf back in elastic band under heading Bills.

Concede I have not accomplished all I had hoped, but have a certain satisfaction in knowing exactly what the problem is.

August 9

Receive telephone call from Beatrice Lawler, asking if she may come over and consult me about a private matter.

Cannot imagine what this means but suspect that some sort of party is in the wind, and unless I keep my wits about me, Beatrice will maneuver me into putting up four unknown friends, to which I shall certainly not consent. Suggest 3 o'clock and she says that she will be here.

Beatrice arrives looking as always very dashing, and wearing a hat with small black veil which covers her eyes and therefore makes it difficult to discover what she is thinking. Am convinced however that it is no party plan that has brought her, for she immediately attempts to close the door of small sitting room. This door always jams, but finally after kicking it several times, I get it shut. (Make mental note to get Mr. Parsons' carpenter to plane down the side.)

Bring out the cigarettes, and Beatrice takes off her hat and moves to the mirror to arrange her already perfectly arranged hair. Standing by fireplace she then announces that she believes her marriage is over.

Am horrified at this statement, for though have never regarded the Lawlers as particularly close, still as neighbors they have been part of the landscape. Ask breathlessly what has happened.

Beatrice produces small handkerchief with which she wipes her eyes, as she says, I don't demand much out of life—all I ask is to be happy.

THE DINNER PARTY

(Think this is quite a tall order but decide to let it go, as do not want her deviated from main point.)

She then lights a cigarette, makes a ring of smoke, and says it is a great relief to talk to me because I am so sensible and have both feet on the ground. (Could really kill her.) A man like Joe, she continues, is very difficult, it sometimes seems as though he went out of his way to be difficult. He simply does not understand her.

As believe that generalities usually cover a specific, ask Beatrice if Joe has fallen in love with someone else. (Sense immediately that this is tactless and should have asked it about her first.)

Beatrice, looking quite startled, replies, Certainly not, though of course I have the Continental Point of View.

I say, Of Course, also, but at the moment cannot quite recall if the Continental point of view means that only the man can have affairs, or both may enjoy them without a fuss.

Tell Beatrice that the reason I am so confounded is that she has always given the appearance of being so extremely contented in her marriage, at which with a wave of her cigarette, and in a rather superior voice, she replies, I hope I am Civilized. (Can think of many occasions, notably when she sings If You Knew Susie, or loses at poker, when she is not civilized at all but decide not to bring That up.)

Beatrice now sits down on stool, half shuts her eyes, and says she will try to give me the picture. For months now, when she has tried to have a real talk with Joe about her feelings and reactions, which are numerous and sensitive, Joe's only response has been to yell at her, You Oughta Take More Exercise, when he knows perfectly well that she has a Thing about exercise. Furthermore Joe has developed an enthusiasm for spending even longer periods of time in the country, when he must realize that she has always had a Thing about the country, except in very limited amounts. But the straw that has broken her poor back is that on the week end when there is to be a Gala at the Club, and before which she had planned to give a little dinner, Joe has invited three old cronies up to play Bridge for forty-eight hours, though he is completely cognizant of the fact that she has a Thing about All of his old cronies.

No one seems to realize, she concludes, that I am Going Mad.

Feel quite stymied on how to make the proper rejoinder, and finally inquire if she has ever considered consulting a Doctor.

Beatrice replies that all her life not only has she had a Thing about Doctors, but also about Dentists.

Deadlock seems to have been reached, and we sit and stare at each other. Finally come right out with it and ask her what a Thing is?

Beatrice, looking astonished, exclaims, Surely you know that. A Thing is a block within you which makes it absolutely impossible for you to take certain actions, or accept certain circumstances, or people. It is Nature's way of protecting the Real You.

Door is now suddenly kicked from the outside, and Cissie demands to enter. On the whole rather welcome this interruption though have to enlist Beatrice's help to open the door from our side where it is badly stuck. After several panting jerks together, and one-two-three PULLS, we finally succeed in getting it ajar.

As I walk with her to her car, Beatrice thanks me with real emotion for the wonderful help I have given her. Then suddenly clapping her hands, she cries she has just thought of a marvelous solution. Why should not she, Charles, and I give a joint dinner at our house before the dance? Tell her quite accurately I have a thing about joint parties.

Charles advises not mixing in one's friends' domestic troubles, but is not above showing considerable interest in what I tell him.

August 12

Rachel returns, with poison ivy on her legs, and filled with enthusiasm for Barker menage.

Listen rather sourly as she describes friend's mother

doing all the cooking which was much fancier than we have, the fun of polishing silver while Brahms Quartet was played on gramophone, and the jollity of picking blueberries.

Charles asks about his opposite number, and is told that he is much younger, and plays the Irish harp.

Linda inquires who got the stockings, and Rachel replies that she gave them to Mother Barker who told her she had pretty manners.

Out of window watch Rachel race down the hill toward the home of the Miss Putnams.

August 14

Kitchen alteration nearing completion and excels fondest dreams. Roza takes attitude that she is responsible for Grand Design and daily lists past horrors that she put up with. Problem presents itself when she places goldframed photograph of her nephew and large bank calendar on mantel of new fireplace, where I had hoped for amusing little French painting, to be picked up for song at some auction. Also refers to kitchen as 'My Kitchen,' and continues to entertain Mr. Parsons and his corps with immense chocolate cakes at round table, while I lack the fortitude to mention price of eggs and heavy cream.

Charles is almost benevolent in his attitude, so grasp

the nettle, show him bank statement and outstanding bills, and beg for his help. With incredible speed he brings order, and am so grateful do not dispute his criticisms as to my methods, and we embark on new plan (the fifth since the first of the year) of household management. New principle introduced that I shall buy no article of clothing out of season, nothing for house unless mutually agreed upon, and tear up all advertisements.

August 16

Linda spends much time in her room, and driving about the country by herself. She does not appear to be moping, but is singularly detached. If Nature does abhor a vacuum it would seem to be there for her to fill, but as she does not, the obligation rests as usual with mother.

Suggest that she invite a few friends in for dinner before the Club Gala. Linda raises her eyebrows and says, You can't, you simply can't be serious.

Point out to her that when one lives in a community, to enjoy it one should Make an Effort, whereupon the eyebrows go a little higher and Linda asks, Why don't you and Daddy go to the party?

Do not particularly like the ironic implication that our presence would be the ultimate example of the grotesque, so reply that we well may, whereupon Charles announces that nothing on God's earth would make him do anything so foolish. Why, he asks, dress up to see a lot of people one sees anyhow, and many others one does not want to see, because of the childish fear that one might be Missing Something.

Charles warms to his theme. Mind you nobody likes a good time better than he, but after all in the country the choice of evening amusements is not particularly stimulating; much better to stay at home and read, etc.

Tell Charles that I have noticed since living in the country an increasing tendency on his part, when nothing better presents itself, to simply go to bed.

Charles says that he Thinks when he is in bed.

August 18

The Mills of the Gods start grinding.

Return from neighboring town extremely hot from a long afternoon of shopping (car as usual piled high with groceries, plus a carton containing twelve heavy bottles which has taken considerable exertion to place on floor by back seat) when I hear Linda's laugh as gurgling as a waterfall. Walk over to where this happy sound emanates, and find her swinging in the hammock with Mr. Dighton of Washington, D.C.

Linda, her cheeks pink, explains that 'Bill' dropped in

(to my certain knowledge she has never seen him before), while Mr. Dighton, practically linking his arm through hers, asks rather fatuously why I hid Cinderella from him.

Charles walks out of the house, looking exceptionally cool, and carrying three juleps, which he carefully places on the ground as he tosses over his shoulder to me that it is lucky I finally arrived as 'We are down to our last half bottle.' Rather pointedly request help in moving the groceries from the car to the kitchen, whereupon Mr. D. exclaims, Beauty we must help Mother. Rapidly figure that though possibly four years my junior, he is undoubtedly twenty years Linda's senior, so tell him a bit tartly that I have had a letter from his friend Julie, to which he airily responds, How is the Old Girl?

Bill, as I now obviously call him, says that he is on his way to Mr. Pullman for the dual purpose of calming him down, while at the same time extracting a large sum of money from him for the Republican National Committee, but, and here he smiles rather sweetly at both Linda and me, there is no hurry.

A julep having revived me, I suggest cordially that he stay for supper. (Think interesting essay could be written on the subject of the hospitality that alcohol almost always engenders.) Linda announces that he Is staying for supper, and also for the night because 'it seemed simpler.' This is one of those ambiguous statements often used to justify anyone in doing anything. She then adds, Now don't fuss Mummie, I have Coped. As am sure that I am the most relaxed of housekeepers, except when driven to the wall, think a rather false picture has been presented of a querulous old body who cannot cope.

Linda wears chintz slacks to supper with the addition of a flower in her hair, which causes Cissie to ask, Why have you put a flower in your hair, and receives the timeless response, delivered in an outraged undertone, Don't make Personal Remarks. Rachel unalerted as to the presence of Mr. Dighton, is dressed in an ancient sailor suit, and must be concluding that for a catch the waters are too riled, for she remains stonily silent with her eyes fixed on her plate.

To establish quite clearly that Bill is after all a friend of Charles and me, ask him for news of Washington.

Washington, Bill replies, is in a state of confusion.

And what of my friend Mrs. Senator Wilkins? Bill has seen Mrs. Wilkins only yesterday and found her rather ruffled, for the Senator is on a Battleship off Cape Hatteras, without her.

Charles asks with surprise what the Senator is doing on a Battleship? Senator Wilkins with two Senatorial colleagues is inspecting the Navy, and, continues Bill, he will probably have an even more inspiring visit than to the

Army Base, for the wily Admirals are all Talleyrands, and past masters in the Art of Influence.

Linda, who is listening with parted lips, declares that all her life she has been passionately interested in the Navy (indeed news to her parents) and also, she adds as an afterthought, in the Senate. Bill lets Linda's eyelash glance play over him, and now addresses his remarks exclusively to her.

The Admirals will take the Senators aboard and display the Fleet in a series of maneuvers, watched comfortably from the Bridge through a spy glass. The air at sea is invigorating, the food is excellent—by far the best of the three Services—and it is after all difficult under these hospitable conditions to even hint at economies. Should Senator Wilkins have the temerity to suggest a reduction in the size of Personnel, he will instantly be confronted with the Marines, and who dares challenge them?

The Navy, Bill concludes, is unbeatable in any engagement.

Linda announces that that is absolutely true, indeed the most interesting thing she has ever heard in her born days, which causes Rachel to lift her eyes from her plate and fix them on her sister with a sardonic expression.

After supper we return to the porch and the atmosphere assumes a pneumonialike temperature, due to the cross currents engendered by Linda's warm responses under Rachel's icy observation. Do not quite see how the evening can be made merry, as feel that conversational topics will soon perish between the zephyr and a small potential tornado.

Bill walks to the end of the terrace with Linda and suggests he give her a little lesson in star gazing—I majored in Astronomy you know. With a great deal of searching of the heavens he finally locates the Big Dipper. Linda asks him if the stars do not make him feel small, and Bill replies Yes, They—and a couple of other things. Linda now almost brazenly begins to recite Star light, star bright, whereupon Cissie, who has been listening intently to her sister, shouts, You can't wish because you aren't looking at the First star. It isn't Fair!

As Linda coils herself for a death-dealing retort, reprieve is sounded by three honks of a horn, and Cissie and Rachel make off for the movies, Rachel however hovering just long enough on the top step to cry *Moonshine* at Linda. This implication is fortunately lost, for Charles has joined the two astronomers, and standing between them, points in all directions as he identifies Mars, Sirius, Dog Star—no, more to the Left, a little further down—and Corona.

Linda replies very sweetly, Yes Daddy, Thank you, Daddy, but Charles is warming up, and seizing her shoulders, says, Now Linda if you will turn around and move over to this side, I will show you Cassiopeia's Chair.

Linda repeats in a controlled voice, Thank you very much Daddy dear but I Know Cassiopeia's Chair already.

Bill lets his eyes roam across the sky again, and exclaims in a disappointed tone, We are too low after all to see glorious Ursa major.

Glorious Who? demands Charles.

If we drove to a higher hill, Linda, we might just catch him. What a celestial planet!

Linda cries, That would be heavenly (her first fairly accurate comment) and this time the arm of Bill is not figuratively linked through hers as they move down the path. As they round the corner Bill calls back to Charles, I hope you don't mind, Sir.

Charles' face undergoes a nervous spasm and he explodes, He called Me Sir!

Tell Charles that Bill is a Rake. We must Do Something. Charles merely repeats in an incredulous voice, Sir.

Say that Bill Dighton is an old roué; look at the way he was with Julie. Now Linda.

Charles paces up and down a couple of times and then tells me to stop being so maternal. Linda and Dighton will sit fleetingly on a rock, and then will go somewhere to get a drink. Linda will tell Bill the story of her life, which fortunately is brief, so they will be home early. Stop worrying. Get a good book and distract myself. He is going upstairs to correct proof.

Rap out that I will not get a good book. If I stay at home, all I will do is listen for the car. I want to go Out to be distracted.

Charles now shows the mark of true greatness. Without further petty argument, he calmly replies Let's go to the Dance.

Am overwhelmed at this understanding and imaginative suggestion. How kind . . . How really touching . . .

Charles says Get Dressed.

In the excitement of this unexpected turn to the evening, and in the fever of fastening a rather complicated pair of zippers on my green dress, do not think about the time, and only as we drive off do I notice on the car clock that it is twenty minutes after nine. As Charles dislikes promptness, but is in so amiable a mood, decide not to irritate him by calling his attention to this, so ask him to drive a little slowly because of my hair. Charles closes the windows. He then says that he is feeling a little tired tonight. It may be that he has been overworking on the book, so do I mind if he does not stay very late at the party? He does not want to spoil my fun, but he himself may slip away.

Assure him that I have no intention of remaining for more than half an hour. We will have a couple of whirls around the floor and leave the moment he wishes . . . I am so sorry that he is tired.

Fortunately there is a line of cars at the Club (showing that we are not the first arrivals), and we have to park a considerable distance from the entrance. On the walk to the door some gravel lodges in my slippers, which makes the trip quite painful, but manage by balancing against Charles to kick out a few of the larger stones.

Agree that we will meet in the Bar, and repair immediately to the dressing room, where I take that long hard look at myself, unavoidable when mirrors reflect all contours and aspects, enlarged and in perspective. First conclusion is that the electric light bulbs at home must be very dim. Decide the green dress is pretty, but naïve, and should be much lower in front. Reinforced in this opinion when three unknown lovelies sail in, burnished and strapless, costumes suggesting Venetian Lido ball.

Sit on chair to shake out last bits of gravel from my slipper and am apparently invisible, for one of the beauties almost sinks down on my lap as she applies two lipsticks of different shades, a rose pink to the upper lip and one of tile red to the lower. Have indeed never seen this before, and watch quite breathlessly the eighteen reflections that are thrown back at me from all sides in A Lip is A Lip is A Lip montage.

Have now such a sense of inferiority, fear that at any

moment one of the charmers may give me a quarter and request her wrap, so ask in a sort of we-girls-together voice, How does the party look?

Utterly ghastly, replies the double lipstick, nothing but playful, shaky old men, and teeny weeny boys.

The three Graces now rise, give a last lingering look at their shining reflections, and swim through the door like three sharks.

Charles is in the bar, a drink in front of him and the tennis Pro beside him. Do not find the records of old matches the most fascinating of topics, but Charles possesses total recall on all the scores of Big Bill versus Little Bill, and the Pro, who can scarcely be more than nineteen and is obviously afraid of Charles, listens respectfully as he sips a coke.

Room begins to fill with a number of young girls and boys and becomes extremely noisy. The presence of the Pro at another table is imperiously demanded by a small sunburned blond, and he rises saying If you will excuse me, Sir. Charles however is undismayed at this designation and signals to Old Tom behind the bar. Am pleased to see that already he appears less tired, but point out that he still has half a drink in his glass, but he observes that with such a crowd it is more efficient to lay in a small supply.

Saxophones sound and after a little persuasion we move

on to the ballroom (gala draped with flags and yellow paper streamers), but the arrangements are changed, for the tables which usually encircle the floor and make a convenient harbor from which to sail out from, or return to, have been removed, and in their place is a long row of little chairs. Charles and I sit down on two of them. The music is exhilarating, orchestra augmented by several drummers, and can see that this is going to be a very good party indeed and that I will not wish to leave at an early hour.

Am determined that Charles shall also have fun, so make a couple of suggestions to him of women whom I think he would enjoy dancing with, such as Maud Tracy (whose feelings would be hurt if he did not), and a nice Mrs. Hilton, who is sitting on the opposite side of the ballroom next to her husband, and who is quite charming in her unaffected Simplicity.

Tell Charles that if he really wishes to do a Kind deed he might also dance once with little Olivia Pullman, as from where I am sitting I can see that she is alone on the porch, and looking rather dismal.

Charles now suddenly sits erect, and asks, Who is That! as he indicates the shimmering figure of the double lipstick, who floats by us resting in the arms of a heavily tanned stranger in a scotch-plaid dinner coat. Cannot identify her beyond saying that I find her unattractive.

[183]

Charles suggests that we dance, and as it is a waltz, the younger people leave the floor in droves, so that we and the others of our generation have a great deal of space. (Am quite aware that it is a symbol of failure to be seen dancing with one's husband, but do not think it appears as too much of a defeat if it occurs early in the evening.)

The orchestra for its next number plays Shady Lady, with a great many drums. Floor immediately fills and I become quite breathless, and finally say to Charles that I will have to sit down. As we watch the dancing, always an entertaining sight, am completely amazed to see Beatrice Lawler glide by with her husband Joe Lawler as partner, on whom she is bestowing the most tender if not passionate of glances through half-closed eyes. But what is equally extraordinary is the costume of Beatrice, for on a summer night she is dressed in a skin-tight black velvet, garlanded in front and in back with marabou.

I ejaculate the single word, Well, and can see that Charles holds the identical sentiment, for his eyes never leave her. Am consumed with curiosity as to what has brought Beatrice and Joe together (if they really are together) and Charles says that he may be able to find out. We get up to dance again, and I am cut in on almost immediately by Mr. Hilton, and in a few seconds by Hick Tracy, and then by Mr. Case. This is gratifying, but recognize that I am spending capital fast, and could wish that my partners were better spaced, or entire fortune will be frittered in a few minutes.

Stroll out with Mr. Case to the terrace to see if I cannot discover some congenial group where the exchange of partners (including the exchange of Mr. Case) may be effected by normal channels, and in spite of the protest of Mr. Case who wishes to discuss Yon Moon, walk to the south side and do find a table where are sitting a couple I know slightly, and several others whom I do not know at all. Stand a bit tentatively near the table which we are rather grudgingly invited to join. Scotch-plaid dinner coat, who is in the shadows, immediately rises and asks me to dance. This is by way of being an extra dividend so do not refuse, and leave Mr. Case on special deposit.

Scotch-plaid says, not very gracefully, Any excuse to get a drink, and moves rapidly to the Bar where he orders a double whisky Quick, then rather handsomely suggests champagne for me. Bar if anything more crowded and so noisy that we have to scream our remarks to each other, but through the din find out that the siren partner with whom I observed him earlier is his wife, she has just had a third child, so he is trying to cheer her up, poor girl. Shout at him that I have three children also. (Think that this is not a very flirtatious opening.)

Plaid now asks me, voice growing very hoarse, if I am

as worried as he is about the stock market. Do I think it it Too High?

Nod my head slowly, take a little champagne, and my ears begin to hum.

Plaid, voice quite foggy, urges me to Look at Rails.

Nod my head more profoundly, and feel the room is very hot.

Plaid, dropping his voice to a confidential but still powerful undertone, whispers, Stocks may go even Higher, which seems to fill him with despair.

Ears now quite audibly buzzing, so say almost feverishly that I Must dance. Air instantly revives me and with it conscience returns, and I look about anxiously for Charles, as fear during sojourn in the bar he may have been waiting impatiently to go home. Can see him nowhere.

Plaid is a muscular dancer, but has a tendency at moments to suddenly lean on me for support, so after two rounds say, Thank you so much Kind Sir (There is something about Plaid that elicits this kind of remark), and make my escape.

Stroll in as casual a manner as possible to the front entrance and peer out to see if, like the Flag, the car is still there. Finally identify it, isolated by gaps on either side, and looking as if moss were growing on it.

Undecided on next move, turn back toward ballroom and immediately run into Plaid, who cries triumphantly,

There you are! Brief separation has made our acquaintance blossom with almost tropical swiftness for he puts his arm embracingly about me, pulls me down onto what might be called a loveseat, and asks huskily, Darling, IS the market Too High? My views on financial situation exhausted, and after short, tense argument, interestedly observed by young couple on opposite sofa, persuade him to return to the bar, alone.

Repair again to the ballroom and dance with a mixed bag for what seems like several hours, winding up with the tennis Pro, who is in top training and very active, which I suddenly find that I am not, so repeat after encore, Thank you so much, Kind Sir. (Seem unable to avoid this objectionable phrase.) Sink down on a chair next an elderly lady, who places a wrinkled hand over mine and cries, Oh that we were young and fancy free.

Rise quickly to my feet again and miraculously Young Hick stands in front of me (wrists sticking out several inches from sleeve), and asks, How about treading The Light Fantastic? We put forth, but as a freighter navigating at its own speed and indifferent to the Marconi rigs about us, through which we plow several times, sowing confusion. The music blessedly ends, and in spite of three courteous claps from my partner's large hands, there is a pause.

No, Young Hick has not seen Charles, not in the Club,

but he did notice a couple sitting on the bench by the second tee, and another pair in back of the bunker down in the sand trap. He offers helpfully—if I am worried—to go out and shout.

Explain hastily that I am not worried. Certainly Not. Let's Dance again. We start once more, Young Hick walking me backwards at a slow-gaited almost funereal pace, when from the doors Charles suddenly materializes, waves triumphantly, and shouts, I have been looking for you Everywhere!

Upon the lapels of his dinnercoat are large tufts of white marabou.

*　　*　　*

Fiction swells with descriptive passages of 'Home from the Ball,' that romantic culmination of a night's festivities. Suggest to Charles that I drive, which I know is mean, but happens to be the way I feel. Charles slows the car to a creep, and then has the effrontery to say that he has only one word for Beatrice Lawler—she is Gallant. Give as ironic a snort as I am capable, whereupon Charles flings his arm about me and bawls out: The Girl I love is on a Magazine Cover; I know they painted her Just-for-Me.

Indignant lights are flashed on in a small house we are crawling by, and a voice yells, Young feller, I'll call the Plise!

Tell Charles furiously that I am going to drive and to Stop the car. We both get out, and a million billion stars look down on us, arched over the sky. A meteor falls. Charles sings softly: I'd Fall in Love, If-I-could-ever-Discover . . . and for no reason at all I am no longer angry, but jubilant. I gaze up through space, space, at planets, constellations, and they do not make me feel small at all, for they are probably dead, and at this moment I have the sensation that I am larger than life.

We drive on, and as we draw up to our door a head pokes out of an upper window, and Linda peers down at us. Oh Mummie I have been so worried about you. Where have you Been!

Tell Charles in a kindly voice to brush his coat, and Charles mutters, That damn dandelion fluff.

August 19

At breakfast Mr. Bill Dighton, after saying good morning to Charles and giving him a cheery look, discerningly asks no questions on the evening's gaieties; and Charles, with equal tact, does not refer to his and Linda's outing. Bill departs for his diplomatic negotiations with Mr. Pullman, and Linda looks so detached, cannot decide if all is over, or a future meeting has been sealed.

Curious result of the night's festivities is to stimulate

Charles, without prior suggestion, into performing a series of dreary tasks, which like the Reformation may bring purification to the Founder, but only induces travail to the unwilling followers.

Charles begins his Salvation in the study. Books to be gotten rid of are pulled out of shelves and left in untidy piles about the floor, and I am requested to arrange to have them given to a library, 'or something' where they will be appreciated. As a matter of fact there may be some valuable editions among them, and I had better look them over carefully.

The generous donation that Charles is prepared to make, includes: Holdsworth's History of English Law—Volumes V, VII and VIII; Annual Report of the Carnegie Corporation—1923; Critique of Couéism—Professor Wolfson, Princeton; The Congressional Record—78th Congress; Salmon Fishing in Norway—Lord Abernathy, 1911; Tales from the Bad Lands—Robinson; and The Economic Impossibility of War—Stratton, 1913.

Stack this collection in an unsteady tower behind the door, and a brilliant idea comes to me which I would gladly give to a publisher if I knew one well enough to get his ear. Let him invent a destructive, odorless book powder, to be included as a dividend with every ten volumes purchased. In a week sales will bubble up like new May wine.

Charles next pulls out from behind the space where the two volumes of the Congressional Record stood a wooden box marked 'Hooks and Screws' and completely filled with keys. Will I sit down with him quietly and explain to him which key is for what, so that he can properly label them? There are I would guess about sixty-five keys.

Tell Charles that I have never seen any of them before, and to throw the whole box away and have done with it. But no man ever relinquishes anything made of metal, and if the metal is in the form of a key, it possesses a peculiar and almost sacred quality.

Charles triumphantly lifts out key which is tagged with the words 'Large Green Trunk,' written in faded pink. We do not possess a large green trunk. He burrows further and finds another marked 'Small Case, Henry.' He studies this for several seconds and finally admits that he does not know who Henry is, or was. A heavy key at the bottom causes him to frown thoughtfully, until, with a happy note in his voice, he announces, I believe it Is the key for the old Barn which was torn down.

All keys are finally returned to the wooden box and put back again on the shelf in the space where the Congressional Record—78th Congress stood, for as Charles explains, Now we know exactly where to find them.

The next goal on the road to redemption takes Charles outdoors, and there is an immediate screech of protest from

Rachel, No, I don't want to whiten the tapes on the court. The lime will get on my dress!

The spirit of the saint is now tried, there is a fall from Grace, division fills the air, and the Market, by far too high, crashes.

Maud comes over in the afternoon and we sit under the trees and discuss the dance. Maud reassures me about the green dress which she says would lose all its style if it were lower in front. It is Not that kind of a dress. Even Hick Jr. had admired it. Tell her quite truthfully Young Hick is a lamb.

Finally ask Maud, not unnaturally, what the real situation is between Beatrice and Joe Lawler.

Maud says she has only one word to describe it—Joe is Gallant.

At this moment there is a wild scream, and Cissie shrieks from an upper window, *Daddy has had a terrible accident!*

In the seconds that it takes me to run to the house, my life passes in review, and I recognize my endless cruelties to Charles, and the nobility, no, greatness of his nature— then find him on my bed, trying to mop up a dark brown pool of liquid from the center of the spread, on which are also laid his clean white shirts, now turning burnt-almond.

Still suffering from shock, fling my arms around him, while begging him not to use the linen towels.

Charles says that he was cleaning his shoes. Have been too nearly widowed to ask him Why he did it on the bed.

August 23

Chauffeur brings a note from Mrs. Estabrook Bromley, inviting us for the week end. She writes that the Honorable Lionel Beckett will be with them, and that he particularly wishes to see Charles. Am mystified by this until Charles explains that Beckett is a client of his Firm, and he undoubtedly forced the Bromleys to ask us—as otherwise Why should they? Agree that I can see no reason.

Study Mrs. Bromley's invitation, and the letter paper, which has a series of symbols in the upper left-hand corner denoting: Telephone (an instrument), Telegraph (wires with birds on them), Station (Choo-choo train), Express (packages), and Road Map. Place called 'Back-Eden.' Cannot decide if this is charming, or ridiculous.

Mrs. Bromley says that it will be very informal and to bring something simple. (I know what That means.) She adds in quotation marks 'plain living, and high thinking.'

Tell Charles that when I visit people like the Bromleys, I expect High Living, and a lot of it, and want no thinking at all.

Charles says that if it were not for Beckett he would prefer to stay at home, regardless, but he supposes that he owes it to his Firm to see him.

Ask Charles what the Hon. Lionel is like.

Charles says He is all right.

Is he handsome?

Charles says that Yes, he supposes so, if I like the type.

Is he married?

Charles now becomes irritated, and wants to know why I need all this passport intelligence when I am going to see him in two days.

Repeat, Is he married?

Charles says that though he saw him for a month in Cairo, and later in London, where he lunched with him frequently at his Club, he never happened to ask him. What difference does it make?

Explain that it is almost the most interesting fact about a man, and what is more, it would not take me a month in Cairo to gain this information, as when I meet a man I know without being told within ten minutes.

Charles looks incredulous.

August 27

To bring 'something simple' takes large valise, medium-sized square bag, and zipper shoecase, for One Never Can Tell. Supposing Mrs. Bromley says, Don't dress for dinner.

That could be interpreted as a print, or a cotton evening, or a short dinner dress. On the other hand, it might mean: I and the others are going to fool you, and wear lovely long gowns, quite décolleté, and Won't you look silly.

And assuming Mrs. Bromley tells me that a few old friends are 'dropping in' to lunch; what is she hinting? That implies I think a linen, or even a gingham. But if she says 'I have some guests for luncheon on Sunday,' it would probably indicate a silk. No, much better to be on the safe side and ready for all contingencies.

Rachel is reminded of an earlier statement 'I love to wash cars' and with good grace lends Charles a hand. We drive off in spit-and-polish condition and within ten minutes are caught in a thunderstorm with lashing winds, and mud splatters the hub, while leaves stick on the windshield. Temperature drops, and I could wish that I had worn something warmer than a sleeveless cotton.

Bags impressively carried away at the front door, and an elderly Irish maid tells us that 'Mr. and Mrs. Bromley are in the Dacha playing Canasta.' She then points through the rain to a very large log cabin, heavily planted in fir trees, to which Charles and I run.

Mr. Bromley welcomes us cordially, and I say brightly that I am afraid we have brought the rain. A group is sitting at the card table and all appear to be drinking glasses of strong whiskey, but Mrs. Bromley as she offers me a glass explains that it is tea served in the Russian manner.

Dacha has icons on the walls, crossed scimitars over the fireplace, and is lit by hanging jeweled lamps, which give a dim glow but are augmented by efficient-looking standing lights with parchment shades decorated with Old King Cole motifs. There is also a bar, a ping-pong table, and a long lucite magazine rack on which are several periodicals including Fortune, The Ladies Home Journal, and U.S. News and World Report.

The Hon. Lionel is distinguished, with a proud expression, but wears his hair so very long that he resembles a rather condescending disciple in the Passion Play. Am not given the opportunity to have that little ten-minute chat, for he immediately seizes Charles and demands that he take a walk with him. Rain pouring down, but Charles is evidently unwilling to admit that he is not equally hardy, and follows Lionel into the storm.

There are cries from the card table, Aren't The British Wonderful about weather, and no one calls attention to the identical vigor of Charles.

Mr. Bromley now sits down beside me and I ask him how he happened to build a Dacha in America. Mr. Bromley pulls his chair closer and says Yes, I am entitled to an explanation. (Cannot see why.)

Many years ago after the First World War, Mrs. Bromley, who had always liked foreigners, made the acquaintance of a young Russian—a Georgian Prince in fact—who had escaped to this country. He was very charming, full of high spirits, and frequently visited the Bromleys.

When they were improving Back-Eden, the problem that was uppermost in their minds was how to achieve a large room for entertaining. The Prince suggested, in fact sold Mrs. Bromley on the idea, that a Dacha would be the solution, for not only would it be a delightful and original addition, but far easier to construct than a Japanese Tea House, which had been Mr. Bromley's suggestion.

Grigo—Prince Grigorieff—had flung himself into the building of the Dacha, and had himself carved, while sitting on the top of a carpenter's tall ladder, the Russian lettering that encircles the cornice. He had been invaluable in finding the icons and the old lamps, and even persuaded a friend to sell the Bromleys the scimitars over the fireplace. When the building was finished, the Bromleys had given a fancy-dress party, where Grigo had led the guests in Cossack dances, and they had all drunk Vodka.

Gradually over the years the Dacha had become a bit more modernized, but as their friends told Mr. and Mrs. Bromley over and over again, it never lost its marvelous Russian character.

Now however, says Mr. Bromley lowering his voice, not only has the world situation changed, but the situation in our country. An incident that disturbed both Mrs. Bromley and himself was a picture that appeared in a number of newspapers, with the heading: Malenkov Entertaining the Members of the Politburo at His Dacha. Grigo had always led the Bromleys to believe that a Dacha was an aristocratic hide-out, almost a Grand Duke's hunting lodge.

Mr. and Mrs. Bromley, after seeing the picture, considered painting *their* Dacha white, and calling it The Play House, but paint will not adhere to rough-hewn logs. They then thought of removing the decorations and naming it Maple Sugar Cabin, but there was the problem of the deeply carved Russian sentiment around the ceiling, and neither could remember quite what it meant. Mrs. Bromley thought it expressed: God Bless our Home, phrased more poetically, but Mr. Bromley had an uneasy recollection that it said: Under This Roof we are All Brothers.

Finally, Mrs. Bromley said: Estabrook, as long as we cannot change the Dacha, and as we have no other large room, we must show courage and Carry On. During the summer months we will keep it as a game room for ourselves and those friends who understand the problem, and for the winter months I think it would be wise, and Kind, to offer it to the village for a Community Center.

And that, concludes Mr. Bromley, it what we have done. On November 1st, we wheel out the Bar, hang an American flag over the scimitars, and there are Y.W.C.A. meetings in the daytime, and square dancing at night.

Sit for a moment pondering the strange dilemma of the Bromleys, and then ask what became of Grigo.

Grigo went off to Pasadena, married money, and according to Mr. Bromley, became quite cheap, and lost all of his old world charm.

High living begins in the bedroom. Bags have been unpacked, and dresses, hanging in big closet, look as though they have been dry-cleaned as well as pressed.

Walnut desk is covered with equipment, all in tooled Florentine leather, and had no idea that for writing a letter so much apparatus was considered necessary. In the center is a large portfolio, lined with moiré, which contains a silken cord. Beside it is a desk blotter (encased in Florentine) which rocks back and forth like a see-saw. A giant letter opener, in the form of a sword, shares its scabbard with an immense scissors, long enough to cut wallpaper. A framed perpetual calendar, in which the month of May is matched to the days of August, stands next to double ink wells on a stand. Beside the ink wells is a cylindrical box which contains two wire clips. There is also a Florentine ashtray with a metal screen top, and a magnifying glass with a leather handle.

The only lacks are pens, ink in the ink wells, and paper.

Bathroom replete with powders, carnation oil, eau-de-cologne, band-aids, and bicarbonate of soda. Sprinkle tub with lavender bath salts, lie in scented water, and for no reason at all am homesick, and wonder if Cissie is missing me, and shall I call her up. Interrupted in these minor-key reflections by bang on door, and Charles announces that he cannot find Any of his clothes.

Hasty search in closet reveals tall chest with 24 small drawers, resembling cabinet in which dentist keeps his tools. Single tie is disclosed in No. 2 drawer, socks in No. 4, evening tie in No. 5, shirts in No. 9 split with No. 11, etc. Charles mutters Why can't people Leave My Things Alone; reassembles haberdashery and places all back in his own bag, and then tells me They are Not to be touched. (Do not see why I should carry housekeeping responsibilities on a visit.) Finally prevail on him to leave damp socks and wet shoes out in the open, and not secrete them in valise.

Charles says that he had a fascinating talk with Lionel on the walk in which he divulged something highly confidential—about The Dollar Pool. (Lift one eyebrow.)

The downstairs of the Bromley house is implacably early American. Ceilings are about six feet high, pewter candlesticks mingle with wooden spread eagles, and spindle chairs are scattered over scatter hook rugs. Cocktails, which are served from a cobbler's bench, are fortunately twentieth century.

Other guests are unknown to me, but after swift glance

decide that dinner dress was happy choice, and that Torea-
dor pants, worn by young lady with red hair, appear inappropriate in juxtaposition to old spinning wheel.

Draw Lionel at dinner who opens by asking if I realize
what tremendously Good Value Charles is. Have never
heard this expression before but assume it is a compliment,
and agree heartily. He continues, You know he is ab-so-
lutely First Class. Nod again modestly, but wish to somehow switch the conversation away from Charles and on to
Lionel himself, and his marital or non-marital status. (Difficult to decide whether his nose in air manner would
charm women. Think probably, Yes.)

Spar for a few minutes more on the qualities of Charles—
frightfully keen on tennis, isn't he—and then decide to Cut
Bait, and ask the Question. Take the plunge and say, And
How is your wife?

There is a moment's awful pause before he replies, Oh
you mean Cynthia, poor girl.

Can only bow my head in apology and say I had not
heard (What?). Lionel continues: Yes, she is living with
her people now in Caithness. I nod again in a rueful sort
of how-nice-for-her-but-sad-for-you manner, and he goes
on: Yes, it has been a messy business and a slow one. I must
say you arrange these things jolly fast Out Here. (What
things?)

All is finally clarified when he adds: Violet and I expect to be married at Whitsun when the decree is made absolute.

Reply, Good, in a heartfelt manner, and change the subject.

At the conclusion of dinner we return to the spinning-wheel room. The rain is still falling, and long discussion takes place between Mr. and Mrs. Bromley as to whether we shall, or shall not, rush out with umbrellas to the Dacha. Idea finally jettisoned by redhead who cries, But it is so cute Here.

Bridge players creep away to second small room, and an even lengthier argument begins between the Bromleys as to whether we shall, or shall not, have a fire. It develops into a debate, we all take sides, and fire lighters ultimately win.

Estabrook Bromley bends down to wooden cradle by hearth and extracts three logs, four large pine cones, and tiny scrap of paper, which he carefully places on the Hessian soldier andirons, and then lights. There is a belch of smoke into the room, Mr. Bromley crouches on the floor and blows—and now a battle rages. Mrs. Bromley moves forward and kicks the wood, Mr. B. cries that she has Spoiled Everything, and Charles injects himself by announcing that all that is required is a back draft. Redhead and I in a chorus demand More Paper, while Lionel comes out with an intricate suggestion that he be allowed to build all over again Norwegian style, with logs placed on end. Unknown man and lady, sitting on two milking stools, say nothing, but wipe their eyes expressively.

Sparks however continue to fly between Mr. and Mrs. Bromley. Mrs. Bromley declares that with all the hunting she has done, the one thing that she Knows is how to build a fire, and what is more with wet wood in the snow, and what is more Estabrook had seen her do it—when he couldn't! Mr. Bromley ignores this taunt, and lying in a horizontal position continues to huff and puff.

Mrs. Bromley now wails accusingly: Estabrook, you should have Bought that Toll House hand-painted bellows —when miraculously there is a crackle, and flames burst out in all directions.

Mr. Bromley is triumphantly lifted to his feet as he explains that it is just a simple matter of Know-How, while Lionel surreptitiously opens three diamond-paned windows.

We now sit in a circle on the spindle chairs, and unknown man, Charles, and Lionel enliven us by statements concerning The Sterling Area and a thing called Terms of Trade, which they chew over and hang onto like bulldogs. Estabrook Bromley throws in the suggestion that we must Watch Steel Scrap (at least I Think that is what he says), and Lionel gives a concise paragraph on the industrial output of forty-three states where he has visited. He winds up in Texas which he appears to know like the palms of both hands, is on intimate terms with every billionaire from Dallas to Houston, and all of them are tremendously Good Value.

Mr. Bromley responds to this by saying, Cotton Futures can expect Hedge Selling.

Know that it is a great privilege to Hear the Men Talk, but room is warm, eyelids heavy, and for a few moments I let nature take its course.

I am aroused by hearing Lionel say: While I was in Chicago I visited the Art Institute again to look at the Seurats. La Grande Jatte is sentimental if you will, but it has great charm.

This is greeted by total silence.

Lionel goes on, Your museums do have some extraordinary new acquisitions—That Tintoretto in Minneapolis, the Caravaggio in Kansas City, and that lovely Tiepolo at Springfield.

The room remains quiet.

It makes travel in America a positive joy, don't you agree, Bromley?

Mr. Bromley gives a terrified nod.

Lionel lowers his voice: Give me your advice. Would it be worth my while to fly to Sarasota to see the collection? I hear there are two rather fine Luinis.

Mr. Bromley retrieves his speech, and croaks out NO!

Ask Charles as we go to bed what is the matter with us all anyhow? Charles reminds me that he Did go to the Exhibition of Japanese Art.

August 28

Sleep fitfully due to large grandfather clock in the hall outside door which gives forth a ping ping ping for the quarter hours, on a deeper note a Bong Bong for the hour, with a continuing background tick tick tick tick, like water dripping from a tap.

Charles finally and triumphantly stops clock entirely (probably by breaking it) at about 4 a.m. and there is a deathly stillness. Ask if he will mention this to the Bromleys, and he says Certainly not, that is the sort of hazard a host must accept.

Have breakfast in bed, largely because I never do at home, and it seems foolish to let the opportunity go by. Coffee is excellent but not quite enough of it. Lie back on pillows and think this is rather pleasant, when Charles appears and says, Get up, we are all going for a walk. Think this a foolish idea but in due course find myself in borrowed shoes, marching through wet woods with Mr. and Mrs. Bromley, Lionel, and Charles.

We are in a happy mood, and Lionel looks in particular harmony with the scene as he strides ahead swinging a stick, with nose really in air. Suddenly he pauses by a little brook which has a tiny trickle, and asks, What is this?

Mr. Bromley explains rather proudly that it is a stream 'on my property,' and adds that he has stocked it with trout.

Lionel stops and gives us a short lecture on the absurdity of believing that there can be trout in the U.S. when anyone, But Anyone At All my dear fellow, is allowed to fish. He describes The Test, and jolly strict they are about it, tells a ghastly tale of being taken on an alleged fishing trip in Maine, and winds up that the Trouble with you Americans is that you simply Do Not understand the sport.

We hang our heads in shame.

A young partridge unfortunately crosses the path, which we instinctively try to hide from Lionel. His eye however is too sharp, and it inspires him to a further reminiscence of a day's shooting in the States, which it had taken him a night's journey to reach, and the Limit of the bag for the day was seven birds! Lionel had tried to explain to his host that in Yorkshire it would not be considered a shoot unless at least 120 birds were bagged, but the trouble was that his host was so frightfully thin-skinned.

Mrs. Bromley murmurs that it is a pity it is out of season, as she would like to have a gun in her hands now.

Lionel looks curiously at the shrubs, peers at a leaf on a branch, and then swinging his stick at a sapling, asks, What tree is that, Bromley?

At this our side closes ranks and as a United People rally to protect Estabrook. We will not let him expose himself to this new danger.

That tree, says Charles, is a Fraxinus niger, found only in this State, and I believe Oregon.

And the northeast side of the West Indies, adds Mrs. Bromley.

Charles puts his hand on the trunk of a tall tree and exclaims: Mr. Bromley, I congratulate you on having so large a Fagus grandifolio. How remarkable.

Mr. Bromley flushes with pleasure.

You can find a few in Minnesota, says Mrs. Bromley.

The Ferruginea species, yes, answers Charles, but this one is unique; and he strokes the bark.

But isn't that a beech? asks Lionel.

I believe that is what you call it Out There, I reply.

Lionel's face turns a little pink and we walk on for a few moments in silence. Finally he wheels around and exclaims delightedly, I believe you are all ribbing me!

August 29

We part from the Bromleys and the Hon. Lionel Beckett, all of us regretful and apparently welded more closely by minor differences. Say to Lionel that I wish him every happiness in his marriage with Violet, and Lionel replies that Charles above everyone must know how fortunate he is.

As we drive home Charles remarks musingly that he had always supposed Violet was Lionel's sister. (Find the reticence of men unbearable.)

SEPTEMBER

September 2

Long-distance call from sister Julie that she is coming for short good-by visit, she does not know quite When, but she simply wants to alert us. This has the effect of making me slightly nervous, as, if alerted, one has ample time to prepare, and what will Julie expect?

Charles says to relax, we can always throw a party together. Charles is in a particularly sunny mood, for the book is practically finished he says, and all that is left is some polishing. He has long technical conversations with publisher on telephone, and usually so conscious of toll operators, he recklessly squanders time by replying to questions from the publisher, 'Let me think about that for a moment,' and then Does Think, then and there, on the Long Distance, while the minutes tick by.

September 5

Charles goes to the city for a few days to look at type, format, binding, etc. which sounds as agreeable as choosing a trousseau.

Ask him if he is going to dedicate book to me and he says, Certaintly Not, it is not that kind of a book. Remind him that I did read it, and did find two errors, and that all he has to say is 'Once Again, with Gratitude.' Charles replies that he is infinitely more grateful to Professor Sniglehone, Dr. Chen Loo, Mr. Osterberg of the Treasury, three ladies who did the typing, and believe it or not the Publisher who came up with one very good suggestion for a cut. (See that I have no chance against this competition.)

September 6

Am sitting under a tree at 10 in the morning idly reading, when Cissie rushes out in flood of tears as she points in an anguished manner to her neck. Rachel follows looking slightly shame-faced, while Cissie sobs, She says I've got a frog In My Throat! Take her on my lap and after my fourth explanation of the expression, illustrated by raucous and strangling chokes which make my larynx ache, she gives a watery smile and says, Do it again.

Linda, attracted by the sound, appears and turns accusingly on Rachel saying, You have bats in your belfry, electricity in your hair, and gas in your—when Miss Mary Singer walks across the lawn, carrying a brief case. Mary Singer has as awe-inspiring an effect on the children as the President of the United States would produce on me, and they greet her with hushed courtesy.

Linda, aware of the impression that Cissie's tear-stained face may give, with great sweetness invites her to drive with her to the Quarry lake for a swim, and includes Rachel, with a meaningful proviso, But You sit on the back seat. Rachel responds, Thank you so much, dear sister.

As they walk away Mary Singer says succinctly, They have had a fight. She then looks at me for a moment, and without any preliminary softening up, throws a bomb in my face by stating: I am making you my co-chairman for the campaign.

Look at her blankly, and she continues: We have only fifteen days to get the name on the ballot.

Tell her I do not know what she is talking about.

With a withering Don't you ever read the papers glance, she asks me if I am aware that there is to be a special election for a congressman? Yes, I am.

Am I aware that Democratic leaders are backing a weak dark horse called Ferny Butler? No, I am not.

And do I know that any man may become a candidate in the race for the Congressional Seat, if a minimum of 5,000 people sign a petition and send it to the State Sec. of State requesting that his name be placed on the ballot? No, I do not.

That is why, concludes Mary S., you and I are backing Edward Brickman.

Say, Oh.

Of course he is not well known, but I feel he has the qualifications, don't you?

Tell Mary Singer I have never heard of him.

Mary Singer looks at me impatiently and exclaims rather meaningfully, Come, Come, Use that brain; you must remember him; why he gave me your name.

My mind now begins to slowly turn over, and suddenly I shriek, It's Ed the sub-contractor! Why he is wonderful! Tell her breathlessly how he removed the grass stain from my dress; recall his economic holding down of expenses in the kitchen, and climax my testimony as to his eligibility by crying that he Is a veteran, and a Tall one. Am still gasping over this incredible news when Mary S. opens her brief case and hands me—as though giving a sixth grader her assignment—a typewritten list, and about a thousand petition papers, as she says briskly in a rather schoolteacher voice: And Now to Work.

Mary Singer is formidable, and knocks over each nine-pin that I set up as an example of my unfitness for the task. (Q.) How can I possibly secure 500 names (which is my modest assignment)? (A.) By perseverance. (Q.) How do I find that many Democrats? All the nice people around here are Republicans. (A.) The only requirement is that the signers reside in the District. They can belong to any party or no party; that is the beauty of it. (Q.) Supposing someone asks me what Ed the sub-contractor stands for? (A.) (delivered in a scornful tone) I must find out. (Q.) Won't the backers of the weak dark horse Ferny Butler stop us? (A.) Let them try! (Q.) How do I start?

Mary S. hands me a fountain pen, points to the first line on a petition blank, and says, Sign there.

The die is cast.

September 7

Am not too happy at the thought of breaking the news of my new career to Charles, but am too busy and too beset to give it much thought.

Telephone to Ed the sub-contractor (find it difficult to say Mr. Brickman, but as a candidate for the U.S. Congress, feel it is his due), and he says Call me Ed, and he will be right over.

Ed confirms my earlier impression of honesty, for he

says quite simply that he Is honest. Is confident that if he gets on the ballot, he can beat the weak dark horse in the primary, and on reflection considers he has a good chance of vanquishing Republican candidate in election. (Had forgotten that this was the end-all of our efforts.)

Inquire a little embarrassedly what he believes in, apologizing for being so personal, and Ed replies that he has a program which he stands four square behind. Hastily try to dash it down as he gives it to me: Big armi, strong alis, lo tarf, rod improvnt, no sel tax, beter rura elec, mor garb dispo plants. . .

Say that all sounds Splendid, and exactly what the state needs. Ed looks pleased, and thanks me rather awkwardly for my help. Linda walks in with large map of the Congressional district, left by Mary Singer, and Mr. Brickman obligingly becomes the sub-contractor and nails it up. Analyze the outline of the district and am happy to find that large shopping town is within its limits, though Army Base is not included. Assess the possibilities with Ed as he advises me on the most salient points of approach.

Linda listens to this, while she meditatively studies the candidate as a geologist surveying an unworked mine. She then turns her gaze away, and looking out of the window to the sky, she sighs that all her life she has had the Dream of working in a primary. Ed replies that that is certainly a peculiar dream for a girl to have, but eyes behind the steel-rimmed spectacles rest for a moment on her upturned face.

Linda, with her lips curved as tenderly as the crescent moon, says softly, I can type.

Decide to begin with the Miss Putnams, and take Rachel with me. The younger Miss Putnam has misplaced her glasses, so shares the elder Miss Putnam's, which pass between the sisters like the eye of Cyclops as they study the petition. Both ladies have an instinctive fear of signing their names to a piece of paper, and make me feel that I am trying to sell them worthless railroad stock. The younger Miss Putnam repeats several times, I don't know; I really just Don't Know, while the elder Miss Putnam shouts, Sister, give me back my glasses! She then holds the paper to her nose, and exclaims, No, I don't trust this— At All!

Describe to them once more the Q of C (Qualities of Candidate) but this is brushed aside as immaterial. The younger Miss Putnam announces that A good name is better than precious ointment, and then adds rather pathetically, And that is all we have.

Am now almost groveling in my apologies, when Rachel by a remarkable stroke resolves their doubts. She screams into the ear of the elder Miss Putnam: You don't Understand. Mummie wants you to Get people to sign. She is putting you On the Committee! At the magic word 'committee' Miss Putnam the elder flushes scarlet with entrancement, while the younger Miss Putnam exclaims elatedly: Sister, we are *On A Committee!*

There is a struggle for the pen, which the younger Miss Putnam seizes, while the elder Miss P. booms out at me, When do we go to the First meeting? Say they will hear from me, leave Rachel and a small package of literature for them to peruse, and somewhat depleted, drive on.

Call next on Mr. Case and receive the salutation, Who knocks at my Postern Gate? to which I reply, A Damsel in Distress. We play this back and forth a few times, and then I pull out my papers, at which Mr. Case flinches. But I have learned a little lesson. Touch in the briefest manner on the cause and the candidate, and go straight to the kernel of the nut, which is the widespread demand for Mr. Case as co-chairman of the committee.

Mr. Case demurs, finally acknowledges that he is a beloved figure 'in our little world,' grants that he also possesses the common touch, admits he has a kind of genius for organization, confesses that the times are out of joint (which is the closest he comes to a political comment), and that yes, he will assist our young friend—what is his name by the way?—in this er-er-venture.

Present him with petition blanks, and move on to large town. De Boss at the Food Specialty Shoppe will not let me finish my reasoned arguments, but simply says Sure,

Sure, Sure, and signs his name with a flourish. Has he friends who would be interested? Sure, Sure. Will he be On the Committee? Sure, Sure, Sure, anything to oblige old customer.

Cannot believe that I have really hit pay-dirt, and become a little cautious. He must be absolutely certain that the signators are citizens. Sure, Sure.

De Boss puts twenty petition blanks under a can of lard, and we turn to the subject of new-type port-salut cheese, just in. Buy two pounds.

Get home rather tired, and find that Linda and the typewriter have vanished. Make myself a solitary cocktail, and sip it in my bedroom. (Is politics making me a secret drinker?)

September 8

Charles returns, and on the whole takes my news rather well, because if I do say so, I am pretty wily in the way I tell him. Hide Congressional district map and other matters, and listen to account of visit to publisher which has gone off extremely well, first printing to be large.

Tell Charles that this must give him great confidence, and I envy him this moment. Dilate on my own lack of assurance and sense of inferiority. Even if I wanted to do something, I would doubt my capacity. I just Don't Believe in Myself.

Charles exclaims that this is Nonsense. I must stop being so humble; no one has more capacity than I. Anything I have a mind to do, I could do.

Describe, perhaps a little sketchily, what Mary Singer has suggested, but (and here I pull the wire and the trap shuts) does Charles really believe in me enough, As He Has Said, to think that I could do it?

Charles says, Yes.

September 9

Disturbed when unknown lady calls me up and says that She is Miss Singer's co-chairman, and may she have my report. Inform her that she must be mistaken, hang up, and telephone Mary Singer who is out.

Visit Mr. L., principal of school, who is almost grave in his approach to the problem. The man we choose must have integrity; now is the time to rise above party affiliations; he thinks well of young Brickman, but—he must talk to him.

Stop in at Mary Jane's Beauty Shoppe and am in quite a different kettle of fish. Antie will vote for a Chinaman if he will get that awful tax off cosmetics and French perfume. It is ruining her business. How does Ed Brickman stand on that one?

Tell her that I have every reason to believe that Ed Brickman is against the tax, but Antie is too smart for me. 'Every reason to believe'—but do I Know? Has he come out and said he will introduce a Bill?

Assure her I will find out immediately, and Antie (who I do think is a pretty disagreeable old girl) cocks her bird-eye and says that my hair looks dry enough to start a bonfire. When am I going to take her special oil treatment? Weakly sign up for one, and Antie, somewhat assuaged, takes a petition blank and repeats that if Ed Brickman will promise to lift the cosmetics tax, she will personally secure the names of 93 beauticians who live in the district. Am so dizzied at this possibility that I offer her a chairmanship immediately. Antie refuses.

September 10

Mary Singer says that I Am the real co-chairman but of course authority must be widely delegated to cover the many segments of this enterprise. (Wish I could spin out the words so smoothly.) She then asks me—rather pointedly —how many signatures I have secured.

Reply evasively that my report is not quite ready.

Wish to consult our candidate concerning his policy on beauticians' tax, so drive over to his headquarters, barn behind real estate office in neighboring town, and find seated at a large table, Linda, who tells me officiously that Mr. Brickman is out on the road today making speeches, but if I will wait a few minutes I may see his assistant. Ask her what she is doing, and she answers that she is 'screening all appointments.'

Finally she points to a door, and tells me in a clinical manner, You may go in now. Find young man in shirt sleeves sitting alone, with feet up on desk, doing nothing, so can only conclude that Linda is feeling her oats and drunk with power. Young man has no views on tax, and is not interested. Visit to headquarters most dispiriting.

Hick Jr. appears at the house in Hick Sr.'s new roadster. He has today received his driving license, and he offers himself and his father's car for the campaign. Gratefully, if a little nervously, accept, and Rachel commands him to take her immediately to the Miss Putnams.

Charles is sitting on the terrace with Dr. Root, who greets me in a friendly manner which surprises me after the contretemps at the Fair. To my astonishment he is presenting Charles with a series of forceful arguments in favor of young Ed Brickman. The doctor is forming a small committee—and he looks to Charles for his good aid.

Charles, feebly, says that he belongs to the opposition party, but Dr. Root replies sternly that the only consideration these days is that strong men be sent to the Congress. One must be independent, says Dr. Root; Look at your good wife.

Charles looks at his good wife, I return his gaze pleadingly, and he finally says: Tell you what, Doc. If you can cure my tennis elbow, I'll sign up.

Inform him that we do not want him on those terms, but he has already rolled up his sleeve, and Dr. Root (who is Not the doctor that we use) is tenderly pressing his muscles.

Invade two garages in the afternoon and no one has heard of Ed Brickman, or the primaries, except for chief mechanic at second garage who is for Ferny Butler. I cry that Butler is a weak dark horse, and he says He don't give a damn, he is for Butler.

Am becoming quite discouraged.

September 11

Make a tentative score of my own personal report, due in three days, and even with the most optimistic juggling, can reach no better figure than 33, but still have team to hear from.

Mr. Case telephones in high irritation and says that his lines of authority are being crossed, and he must protest. No one is more forbearing than he, but he will not permit names which rightfully belong to him to be stolen from under his nose. If this goes on, he must regretfully resign.

Ask agitatedly what has happened.

Mr. Case explains that for years he has given his trade

to the Groves Green Houses, in fact Mr. Groves has often consulted him, cognizant of his vast knowledge of Floribunda. Yesterday Mr. Case went to the green houses, aware of the many men that Mr. Groves employs, and there he found the Putnam sisters, who had driven over in young Hickman Tracy's car, going through the glass houses, With Petition Blanks!

When Mr. Case objected strenuously, as he felt he had every right, the younger Miss Putnam had darted ahead to the cold frames on the outside to reach two men who were stacking manure, while the elder Miss Putnam had almost physically blocked him, as she yelled—and there is no other word to describe it—We are On the Committee. Mr. Case had no desire to become part of a brawl, so he had withdrawn to Mr. Groves' office, and lo and behold, the young secretary, Miss What's-her-name, had held up some further petition blanks and informed him that the Miss Putnams had invited her but e'en now to be on the committee, and she was honored.

Either I am the chairman, or I am Not the chairman, Mr. Case ends bitterly.

Assure Mr. Case that he Is the chairman, and promise that all names, save those few collected by the Miss Putnams, shall be part of his report. Somewhat mollified, though still distant in manner, Mr. Case hangs up.

Receive a thrilling visit from de Boss himself, who

drives over in his delivery wagon. He brings eleven petition blanks filled with signatures which look bona fide
as each one is in a different handwriting. Says he had to
get a little rough with those Crazy Women who live on
Olive Street. (Have never heard of Olive Street.)

He suggests that Ed Brickman come to his store on
Saturday when he is having his big Sale, and shake hands
with the customers. Tell him I will take it up with Mr.
Brickman immediately; and does he want some more
blanks? Sure, sure, plenty more little birds in the trees;
and would I like some more Domestic port salut? Sure,
sure, and I buy three pounds.

Cissie will not kiss Charles goodnight, but kicks him
in the ankle hard because he won't help Mummie. Charles
says his home is being destroyed.

September 12

Go into kitchen to plan meals, and find Mr. Parsons
drinking coffee, though work is completely finished. As he
has been most unco-operative in campaign, am quite chilly
to him. Roza says Broilers, and comes up with no further
ideas. Asks me what on earth she is supposed to do with
all that cheese. (Is Roza having a collapse?)

Meet Charles on the stairs carrying five Hong Kong
shirts. Says he is driving over to Chinese laundry, if I think

shirts will be safe there. Reassure him by telling him that since departure of Toona have tried Chinese laundry and pleated silk dress came out well.

Charles then makes a surprising gesture. Asks for a petition blank, and says he will try to pick up a few names at the laundry. But I am not to think he is doing this because his tennis elbow is cured, because it is not—he simply wants To Help Me. Tell Charles that this is his finest hour, and I will never forget it.

September 14

Mary Singer's meeting takes place on the lawn in back of her house, and all local teams are present. We sit with our groups facing a card table on which is a large basket decorated with red, white, and blue ribbons.

Mary S. welcomes us in a brief and rather businesslike way, showing that this is no afternoon for pleasure, and then, rapping on the table, calls on us compasslike for our reports. Fellow workers, she cries, we will first hear from North.

North rises from the ground, stout lady in green hat, and announces that with two teams still to hear from, she is happy as of today to bring 843 names. We all applaud as she dramatically places her petitions in the basket.

South is next, elderly man with sunglasses, who says:

Madam Chairman, for the petition to go to the Secretary of State to place the name of Mr. Edward Brickman on the ballot for the special election of a Congressman representing the 28th District (deep breath), South brings you today 920 signatures, garnered by seven teams, and South is not finished! We all cheer as South marches forward and places his petitions in the basket.

Mary Singer now turns to East, and East, represented by a young woman in a pink sweater suit, makes the shameful statement that she misunderstood the directions, and has brought only her own collection of 31 names. These are placed in the basket in total silence, and Mary S. after a short pause requests her to bring all signatures tomorrow, Without Fail, which East, looking quite pale, promises to do.

Mary Singer now orders The Report from West. Mr. Case and I both rise, and I say a little haltingly, but rather graciously I think, that Mr. Case will give the first figures. Mr. Case announces in a low but vibrant voice: I and my assistants bring you today 878 signatures. As the applause begins, I raise my hand and request the Miss Putnams to stand up.

The two Miss Putnams are dressed to kill in ancient flowered hats and beautifully pressed white cotton dresses. Both have their spectacles, and after a little argument the younger Miss Putnam seizes the initiative, and reads from a small piece of paper: I bring you today four petitions duly endorsed by 37 names, and I would like to say—when the elder Miss Putnam, fairly trembling with excitement, interrupts: And I bring you twelve petitions with 120 names! She then waves her papers triumphantly at us, including that special blank signed by those crazy women on Olive Street.

The sisters march forward, accompanied by waves of applause, and place the petitions in the basket, and Mr. Case behaves extremely well and wrings their hands.

But we are not allowed to taste these fruits of victory for long, for Mary Singer makes a speech berating us. This is all very well, she says, but we are not yet Over the Top. Time is short; we must redouble our Efforts. It is Later than we think. Look at This, she cries, and holds up a leaflet printed with heavy brown letters; this is a Ferny Butler petition, and they are flooding the District! We growl like a Roman mob, and almost shake our fists.

And now Ladies and Gentlemen, Mary S. concludes in a milder voice, we will hear from Our candidate.

Ed Brickman on a different note says that what we are doing Is tremendous and our achievements Are remarkable, and that if his name is on the ballot he knows that he can defeat Ferny Butler. He then shakes one and all by the hand, and we vow with fervor we will Get More Names.

Dr. Root springs up and reminds us of the coming Rally. It is of paramount importance that we are all there, for both candidates will be present. Let our voices be heard.

Meeting ends with orange juice and Nabiscos. South and I analyze techniques, and East is treated like a leper. Rachel, face purple with pride, sits between the two Miss Putnams.

September 16

Mary Singer and I hold strategy meeting with Ed Brickman, and Linda at the last moment slides through the door, holding pad and pencil.

Candidate proves stubborn and refuses to accept some extremely valuable suggestions. Ed does not want his war record mentioned again, now or later. It is, he says, a cheap way to win. Furthermore, he refuses to come out for a higher tariff on imported felts for hats, though if he would do so Mary S. says that head of largest hat factory guarantees big block of votes.

And lastly, Ed believes in a higher tax on powders and perfumes. All these idle women who spend their lives getting their hair and faces fixed up instead of minding their homes should be made to realize that a Beauty Parlor is a luxury, and it should be so classed.

At this last statement Linda almost faints, as she gasps, That is not true; a beauty parlor is a Necessity!

Ed, who I think is very tired, gives a shrug, while Linda stares at him as though a Ming vase had crashed to the floor.

September 18

Rally is scheduled for 7 p.m., but in my anxiety that I shall not be late, arrive at 6:15 and have to wait outside Odd Fellows Hall for the back door to be unlocked. Have not told Charles the big surprise which is that I am sitting On the platform.

Dr. Root appears, and two unknown women join us, who, Dr. Root whispers, are probably from the Ferny Butler camp. Whisper back that just by looking at them I would have guessed! Walk around to the front and find doors open and a number of people already filing in. Do not wish to be seen as I am after all an official tonight, so return to back door which remains sealed. Dr. Root says that this is outrageous and he is going To Do Something. He disappears, whilst the two women and I stand glaring at the door.

Sound of music now comes from the inside, and is followed by the stamping of feet. Press my ear to the door and think I hear a tenor voice. Ask one of the ladies rather despairingly What she thinks can have happened? Lady replies that what has happened is that the door is locked.

Time is passing and I become more agitated. There is now silence from within, so choose the moment to make myself heard, and kick the door several times. One of the ladies says that I wouldn't do that if I were you—someone is giving the Invocation.

Rush to the front again and crowd is so great that I can hardly wedge myself into the hall. Finally achieve this by pushing hard, and as I squeeze in I hear speaker on the platform, which is completely filled by notables sitting in two rows, requesting us to all join him in singing Onward Christian Soldiers.

Under cover of this stirring hymn, weave my way toward the platform and ultimately reach it. Seat is found for me in back row, and I sink down without daring to raise my eyes. In a moment however I realize that no one is looking at me at all, for there is a commotion in the back of the hall. Eyes leave the platform, heads turn, there is a murmur which rises to a crescendo, and as the martial strains of the last verse sound out, the weak dark horse lopes up the aisle.

Ferny Butler, who is stout and has a great many black curls, receives a standing ovation, and perforce the Brickman backers also get up, but do not applaud. Am pained at the sight of Cissie, who is with Charles in the fourth row, on her chair and cheering. Think Charles could at least pull her down.

An angular lady presents the candidate. After a preamble, which touches on a number of unrelated subjects, she announces: And so I give you One we can trust, and One we can love—A Reel YOOMAN BEE-EN—FERNY BUTLER!

Mr. Butler steps forward and rolls out that this is the proudest moment of his life; he is profoundly moved by this show of confidence from friends, fellow Americans, whom he wants to serve. He describes in general terms how he will serve—By Scrutinizing—By Demanding—and gives us a definition of his philosophy: When I was but a small lad, me father taught me something which has been me guiding principle throughout the years. Son, he said to me, Son, Be a Good Sport, and you will win the Biggest Game of All.

Angular lady cries out that it is heart-warming for us all to have this shared experience; God bless Ferny Butler, and God bless his Grand Old Dad! Audience responds by singing God Bless America.

South, still wearing his sunglasses, now steps forward. He would like to remind us that we are not gathered together for a song fest, but for the serious business of considering the qualities of a candidate for the United States Congress. He hopes that we are worthy of this responsibility. Having shot out this spray of cold water over the audience, he says quite simply: Ladies and Gentlemen, let us hear from Edward Brickman.

Ed, who is sitting in the back of the hall, rises, and some instinct makes his backers refrain from applause as he walks up the center aisle. This contrast to the entrance of Ferny Butler is marked, and has a touch of the dramatic which is not lost on the audience.

Ed looks through his glasses for a moment at the up-turned faces, and then says that he is a building contractor, so he will talk in those terms. To build well, you must have your specifications, and you must live up to them. He will tell us what his specifications will be if he is nominated for the Congress.

Ed pours out more steel and concrete in our defense, he lowers a wall called tariff which is too high between us and our neighbors, he suggests that the wires which have short circuited in the Attorney General's office be replaced . . . but he has a bear by the tail with these metaphors, and becomes entangled by them. As his nervous adherents listen to him flounder in a flight of imagery—more bricks in the chimney of farm support prices—the audience begins to laugh. But by that mysterious alchemy which can win an assembly, Ed's rather desperate symbols are nevertheless converting the crowd over to his side, and there are scattered hand claps.

Ed smiles, and says he guesses he had better throw away that fancy blueprint and just talk, which he does in a clear and factual way, for ten minutes. At the conclusion of his peroration 'Thank you a lot for listening to me, well, good night,' he receives rounds of applause throughout the hall, and a small ovation from his closely-knit followers. Cissie is on her chair again cheering, and Charles is waving—I think at me.

As I start clambering down from the platform, ask Mary Singer what she thinks. Has Ed a good chance for the ballot? Mary S. looks at me pityingly and says, He had 5,000 names ten days ago, it is over 8,000 tonight, 'but I didn't want my workers to let up.' Tell her furiously that co-chairmen are Not workers. Mary S. pats me on the back and says that if I had walked around to the opposite side of the hall this evening, I could have come in through the regular back door With the co-chairmen. Why do I never use that brain?

September 20

Julie telephones that she will arrive tomorrow, at the same air field, at the same time—Darlings, I can't wait to see you all!

Charles agrees that we must give her a party, but not to have it on a Saturday as Old Tom will be busy at the club. Ask Charles whom we shall invite, and after several moments of pondering, he suggests that we have someone we really like—why not Maud and Hick Tracy?

I suggest that we make it an occasion for Linda also before she returns to college, and Charles replies by all means, he will wear his flowered waistcoat, and we can dance. Tell him that we must then find two attractive single men, and Charles says to leave all that to him, he will attend to it. Am stunned with gratitude and surprise.

We pull a rug out into the sun, and Taffy and Old Joe join us. Autumn is in the air and I ask Charles if he finds it as sad as I, to have the summer over. Charles answers that on the contrary he prefers the autumn to all seasons, it is to him like the opening game.

Say that the turn of the year makes me take stock, and as I look back I find so many people and events are unresolved. For instance, Ed. So far so good, but what will happen from here on out is still the great gamble. And what about gallant Beatrice and gallant Joe Lawler? No bang at all. In a book there is a beginning, a middle, and an end; but in real life . . .

In real life, says Charles, it is never quite resolved.

But Linda, I persist, what about Linda?

If I am interested, Charles replies, yesterday Linda received two telegrams from Bowie Norman. Rachel of course was my informant.

But what is she thinking? That is what I never know.

Charles answers that I should thank my lucky stars that Linda's thoughts are inconclusive.

Chew some grass, look up at the turning leaves, and repeat that I wish there was a finale, a climax to the summer which would be as inevitable as the fall of the apples from the trees. As I say these words two large shadows cross the rug, and Mr. and Mrs. Pullman stand before us.

We have come, says Mrs. Pullman, to say Farewell.

Charles and I express surprise and regret that they should be leaving. Are they returning to the city?

Mr. Pullman clears his throat: Yesterday I received a telephone call from Washington—when Mrs. Pullman interrupts; George Pullman has been appointed Chairman of a Committee to study Procurement Procedures for the Department of the Interior! Isn't that what it is called, George?

We congratulate Mr. Pullman, and Charles says that he knows of no one who will do a more constructive job.

Mr. Pullman answers that it will entail a considerable personal sacrifice, but if one is requested to head up a Task Force, in these days how can one refuse?

Charles agrees that he must indeed accept this responsibility, and then in a burst of warmth suggests that if this assignment does not begin immediately, will not Mr. and Mrs. Pullman come to a dinner party?

Mr. Pullman says that Alas, he is even now on his way to catch the plane for Washington. His face takes on a deeper glow as he adds, Tonight I am attending a stag dinner at the White House.

But you Mrs. Pullman, Charles insists before I can stop him, we want You.

If you do not mind an extra woman, Mrs. Pullman replies, I will come.

Give Charles an eloquent look.

Charles goes off to investigate new pick-up truck, and I lie back again on the rug, and look up at the trees. What shall I give our guests for dinner? What new creation of nectar, hummingbirds' tongues, will come to me for Julie's party?

Gaze at the red leaves for inspiration when suddenly wild laughter comes from the kitchen, and I hear Cissie cry out in ecstasy, You must wear a white veil! This is followed by the sound of weeping, and Roza sobs, My tears, they are the tears of joy.

Bury my face in my arm, and would like to bury my body in the earth as Cissie shouts, Come Quick, Everybody. It's Roza's Secret. Guess what she is going to do!

Like Greek tragedy I know what the gods have in store

for me, and that it was so destined on that summer's day, when I tampered with a fortune.

*   *   *

An apple falls.

GRETCHEN FINLETTER

Through inheritance and by marriage, Gretchen Finletter lived in many worlds. Daughter of Walter Damrosch, she grew up in New York and attended private schools with her three sisters, meanwhile living at home in an atmosphere of music and gaiety. The recollections of those years were set down in a charming book, *From the Top of the Stairs*. Mrs. Finletter, who made her home in New York, travelled all over the world with her husband, Thomas K. Finletter, while he was Secretary of the Air Force during the Truman Administration and, later, Ambassador to NATO.

Gretchen Finletter died in 1969.